DATE DUE

DEMCO 38-296

The Ch'i-lin Purse

THE Ch'i-lin Purse

A Collection of Ancient

Chinese Stories

RETOLD BY

LINDA FANG

PICTURES BY

JEANNE M. LEE

A SUNBURST BOOK

FARRAR STRAUS GIROUX

AUTHOR'S ACKNOWLEDGMENTS

I want to thank my father, Joseph Fang, for guiding me tirelessly through my research on the original Chinese texts. Also, I wish to express my profound gratitude to my friends Lawrence Yep, Pat Markun, and Robin Moore; to my former English professor John Hirsh, who encouraged me to write the book; to my friend Jeanne Casey and my sister Helen, who edited the first few drafts of my manuscript; to my niece Elizabeth Rose, who assisted me in romanizing the Chinese names and place-names; and, inspired me to go back into the treasure house to search for more treasures, to Jeanne M. Lee for her beautiful artwork, and to my agent, Barrie Van Dyck, whose advice played a crucial role in this project.

Distributed in Canada by Douglas & McIntyre Ltd.
Printed in February 2011 in the United States of America
by RR Donnelley & Sons Company, Harrisonburg, Virginia
Designed by Lilian Rosenstreich
First edition, 1995
Sunburst edition, 1997
15   17   19   20   18   16   14

Library of Congress Cataloging-in-Publication Data
Fang, Linda.
The Ch'i-lin purse : a collection of ancient Chinese stories /
retold by Linda Fang ; pictures by Jeanne M. Lee.
p.   cm.
Contents: The Ch'i-lin purse—Dog steals and Rooster crows—The two
Miss Peonys—The Ho-Shih jade—The Prime Minister and the General
—The clever magistrate—Mr. Yeh's New Year—The miracle doctor
—The royal bridegroom.
ISBN: 978-0-374-41189-3 (pbk.)
[1. Takes—China.   2. Folklore—China.]   I. Lee, Jeanne M., ill.
II. Title.
PZ8.1.F19Ch   1994   [398.2'0951]—dc20   94–9909

*For my dear parents, who led me into the
treasure house of ancient Chinese stories*
— L. F.

For Mimi B. Solomon
— J. M. L.

Contents

Author's Note

When we were children growing up in Shanghai, our greatest treat during vacation time was to listen to our mother telling stories. Every evening after supper, my sisters, my brother, and I would gather around and wait patiently for her to finish reading a chapter or two of an exciting novel. When she had finished, she would close the book, put it aside, and then tell us the story from memory.

She was such a wonderful storyteller that all the characters in the book—heroes, villains, emperors, high officials, beautiful maidens, and handsome young men, as well as simple, honest folk—came to life. One of the stories she told was "The Ch'i-lin Purse." This heartwarming story about two brides who were married on the same day touched me deeply and has stayed with me ever since. And so it has become the title of this collection.

When I was about eight years old, my father introduced me to classic Chinese novels. These novels, written mostly during the Ming Dynasty (1368–1644), were based on *hua-pen*—storytelling scripts that were handed down from the Yüan Dynasty (1271–1368).

One afternoon, as I was taking a nap on a bamboo mat, I suddenly felt my father's hand tapping me on the shoulder. "Time to read, get up!" he said. I opened my sleepy eyes and sat up. He was holding a book entitled *Shui-hu* (*The Outlaws of the Marsh*). Sentence by sentence, he read and explained the first chapter to me. I was fascinated by the hero and could hardly wait for my father to continue the next day. After a few of these sessions, I started to explore the novel on my own. It was written in a kind of Chinese language that was used several hundred years ago, and even though many words and phrases were unknown to me, I was somehow able to finish the book and understand most of what I had read. This was the first of many classic Chinese novels that I have read and enjoyed over the years.

When I was a little older, I fell in love with *Hsi-ch'ü*—Chinese opera. This is a general term for an art form that includes Peking opera, Yüeh opera, and other regional operas. This tradition, which started in the T'ang Dynasty (618–907) and flourished in the Yüan Dynasty, evolved over more than a thousand years. Peking opera is about two hundred years old and Yüeh opera about half that. While the melodies and singing styles differ from one kind of opera to another, the costumes, makeup, props, gestures, and *wu-kung* (martial arts) are quite similar. Beautiful stories, both happy and sad, are told by actors through their graceful movements and melodious songs.

As a professional storyteller, I have taken my repertoire from my favorite Chinese novels and operas. I have also used many stories based on actual historical events. However, because of the time constraint on live performances, interesting details always have to be omitted. Therefore, it has been my wish to share these stories in written form with my American friends. This book is my dream come true.

The Ch'i-lin Purse

The Ch'i-lin Purse

It is said that many years ago in China, in a small town called Teng-chou, there lived a wealthy widow, Mrs. Hsüeh. She had only one daughter, Hsüeh Hsiang-ling. Hsiang-ling was beautiful and intelligent, and her mother loved her dearly. But since everything Hsiang-ling wanted was given to her, she became rather spoiled.

When Hsiang-ling was sixteen years old, her mother decided that it was time for her to marry. Through a matchmaker, Hsiang-ling was engaged to a young man from a wealthy family in a neighboring town.

Mrs. Hsüeh wanted to prepare a dowry for Hsiang-ling that no girl in town could match. But Hsiang-ling was hard to please. Almost everything her mother bought for her was returned or exchanged at least two or three times.

When the dowry was finally complete, Mrs. Hsüeh decided to add one more item to it. It was the Ch'i-lin Purse, a red satin bag embroidered on both sides with a *ch'i-lin*, a legendary animal from ancient times. The *ch'i-lin* had scales all over its body and a single horn on its head. In the old Chinese tradition, the *ch'i-lin* is the symbol of a promising male offspring. Mrs. Hsüeh wanted to give Hsiang-ling the purse because she hoped that her daughter would give birth to a talented son.

When the purse Mrs. Hsüeh had ordered was ready, a family servant brought it home. But Hsiang-ling was not satisfied at all. "I don't like the pattern, take it back!" she said.

The servant returned to the store and ordered another. But when it was brought home, Hsiang-ling merely glanced at it and said, "The colors of the *ch'i-lin* are too dark, take it back!"

The servant went to place another order, but the new purse still did not please her. This time the servant broke down in tears.

"I won't go back again, young mistress. The people in the store laugh at me. They say I am hard to please. This is not true. You are the one who is hard to please.

If you don't want this purse, I am going to leave you and work for someone else."

Although Hsiang-ling was spoiled, she was not a mean-spirited person. She somehow began to feel sorry for the old man, who had been with her family for more than forty years. So she looked at the purse and said, "All right, I will have this one. You may go and pay for it." The servant went back to the store, paid for the purse, and gave it to Mrs. Hsüeh.

Hsiang-ling's wedding fell on the eighteenth day of the sixth month according to the lunar calendar. It was the day Hsiang-ling had longed for since her engagement. She was very excited and yet a bit sad, because she knew she was leaving her mother and the home she had lived in for sixteen years.

Hsiang-ling wore a red silk dress and a red silk veil over her head. As she sat in her *hua-chiao*, a sedan chair draped with red satin, and waited to be carried to her new home, her mother came to present her with the Ch'i-lin Purse.

"My dear child," she said as she lifted up the satin curtain in front, "this is your *ta-hsi-jih-tzu*, your big, happy day. I am delighted to see you get married even though I will miss you terribly. Here is the Ch'i-lin Purse. I have put some wonderful things in it. But don't open it now. Wait until you are in your

5

new home, and you will feel that I am with you."

Hsiang-ling was hardly listening. She was thinking about the wedding and wondering about her husband-to-be, whom she had never met. She took the purse and laid it on her lap. A few minutes later, four footmen came. Picking up the *hua-chiao*, they placed it on their shoulders, and the wedding procession began.

As the procession reached the road, it started to rain. Soon it was pouring so heavily that the footmen could not see well enough to continue. The wedding procession came to a halt, and the *hua-chiao* was carried into a pavilion that stood alongside the road.

There was another *hua-chiao* in the pavilion. It was shabby, with holes in the drapes. Hsiang-ling could hear a girl sobbing inside. This annoyed her, because she believed that a person crying on her wedding day could bring bad luck. So she told her maid to go and find out what was wrong.

"The bride is very sad," the maid said when she returned. "She is poor and has nothing to take to her new home."

Hsiang-ling couldn't help feeling sorry for the girl. Then her eyes fell on the Ch'i-lin Purse in her lap. She realized that she was lucky to have so many things, while this girl had nothing. Since she wasn't carrying any money with her, she handed the Ch'i-lin Purse to her maid. "Give this to the girl, but don't mention my name."

So the maid went over and gave the purse to the other bride. The girl stopped crying at once. Hsiang-ling had given away her mother's wedding gift without ever finding out what was inside.

A few minutes later, the rain stopped, the footmen picked up Hsiang-ling's *hua-chiao*, and the procession continued on its way. In an hour, Hsiang-ling arrived at her new home. She was happily married that evening, and to her delight she found her husband to be a wonderful and handsome young man. In a year's time, when she became the mother of a little boy, she felt she was the happiest woman in the world.

But six years later, there came a terrible flood. Hsiang-ling and her family lost their home and everything they owned. When they were fleeing their town, Hsiang-ling became separated from her husband and young son in the crowds of other townspeople. After searching for them in vain, Hsiang-ling followed a group of people to another town called Lai-chou. She had given up hope that she would ever see her husband and child again.

As Hsiang-ling sat, exhausted and alone, at the side of the road leading to Lai-chou, a woman came up to her and said, "You must be hungry. Don't you know that a *li* down the road there is a food-distribution shack? Yüan-wai Lu has opened it to help the flood victims. Talk to his butler. I am sure you can get something to eat there.''

Hsiang-ling thanked the woman, followed her directions, and found the place. A long line of people with bowls in their hands were waiting to get a ration of porridge. Hsiang-ling had never done such a thing in her life. As she stood in line holding a bowl and waiting her turn, she felt distraught enough to cry, but she forced herself to hold back the tears.

Finally, when it was her turn, Yüan-wai Lu's butler scooped the last portion of porridge into her bowl and said to the rest of the people in line, "Sorry, no more porridge left. Come back early tomorrow.''

The person behind Hsiang-ling began to sob. Hsiang-ling turned around and saw a woman who reminded her of her mother, except that she was much older. Without a word, she emptied her porridge into the woman's bowl and walked away.

The butler was surprised at what Hsiang-ling had done. Just as she had made her way back to the road, he caught up with her and said, "Young lady, I don't understand. Why did you give away your porridge—are you not hungry?''

"I am hungry," said Hsiang-ling, "but I am young and I can stand hunger a bit longer.''

"You are very unselfish," said the man. "I would like to help you. My master, Yüan-wai Lu, is looking for someone to take care of his little boy. If you are interested, I would be happy to recommend you."

Hsiang-ling gratefully accepted his offer and was brought to the house where Yüan-wai Lu and his wife lived.

Yüan-wai Lu, a man in his early thirties, was impressed with Hsiang-ling's graceful bearing, and he agreed to hire her. "My wife's health is very delicate and she seldom leaves her room. Your job is to take care of our son. You may play with him anywhere in the garden, but there is one place you must never go. That is the Pearl Hall, the house that stands by itself on the east side of the garden. It is a sacred place, and if you ever go in there, you will be dismissed immediately."

So Hsiang-ling began her life as a governess. The little boy in her care was very spoiled. Whenever he wanted anything, he wanted it right away, and if he didn't get it, he would cry and cry until he got it. Hsiang-ling was saddened by his behavior; it reminded her of how spoiled she had been as a child.

One day, Hsiang-ling and the little boy were in the garden. Suddenly, the ball they were playing with disappeared through the window of the Pearl Hall. The boy began to wail. "I want my ball, I want my ball! Go and get my ball!"

"Young Master, I cannot go into the Pearl Hall,"

said Hsiang-ling. "Your father doesn't allow it. I will be dismissed if I do."

But the little boy only cried louder, and finally Hsiang-ling decided that she had no choice. She walked over to the east side of the garden and looked around. No one was in sight. She quickly walked up the steps that led to the Pearl Hall and again made sure that no one was watching. Then she opened the door and stepped in.

She found herself standing in front of an altar, where two candles and some incense sticks were burning. But in the place where people usually put the wooden name-tablets of their ancestors was the Ch'i-lin Purse! Instantly she recalled the events of her wedding day and how happy she had been. She thought of her wonderful husband and her own son and how much she missed them. She had had everything then, and now she had nothing! Hsiang-ling burst into tears.

Suddenly, she felt a hand on her shoulder. When she turned around she found herself face-to-face with Mrs. Lu, her mistress, and a young maid.

"What are you doing here?" Mrs. Lu asked angrily.

"Young Master told me to come here and pick up his ball," Hsiang-ling replied.

"Then why were you weeping at the altar?"

"Because I saw the purse that once belonged to me."

Mrs. Lu looked startled. "Where are you from?" she

asked, as she took the purse from the altar and sat down on a chair that leaned against a long table. There was a tremble in her voice.

"I am from Teng-chou."

"Bring her a stool," said Mrs. Lu, motioning to her maid. Not wanting to wait on another servant, the maid grudgingly brought a stool and put it to Mrs. Lu's right. "You may sit down," said Mrs. Lu. Somewhat confused, Hsiang-ling sat down.

"What was your maiden name?"

"Hsüeh Hsiang-ling."

"When were you married?"

"On the eighteenth day of the sixth moon, six years ago."

"Bring her a chair and put it to my left," Mrs. Lu ordered her maid. Hsiang-ling was told to move to the chair. She was surprised to see herself treated as a guest of honor.

"Tell me how you lost the purse," said Mrs. Lu.

"It was a gift from my mother. My wedding procession was stopped on the road because of a storm, and my *hua-chiao* was carried into a pavilion. There was another *hua-chiao* in it, and the bride was crying."

"Move her chair to the middle and move mine to the right side," ordered Mrs. Lu. The chairs were switched, and once again Hsiang-ling was told to sit down. She was astonished to find herself sitting in the middle seat—the place of the highest honor.

"Please continue," said Mrs. Lu.

"I gave the bride my purse. I never saw it again, and I have no idea how it got here."

Mrs. Lu dropped to her knees in front of Hsiang-ling and cried, "You are my benefactor! All these years I have been praying here for your well-being. When I got to my new home, I opened the purse and found it full of valuables, including this." She opened the purse and took out a piece of jade. "My husband and I were able to pawn it for a large amount of money. Using the money, we started a business and have now become very wealthy. So I reclaimed the jade and have kept it in the purse since. We also built the Pearl Hall to house the purse and to honor you.

"I knew that you lived in the Teng-chou area, so when I heard about the flood I prayed day and night in that direction, begging Buddha to protect you from harm. I was hoping that one day I would find you and show you my gratitude. And here you are, taking care of my son! I know what we must do. We shall divide our property and give you half of it. That will make us all very happy."

Hsiang-ling was speechless as Mrs. Lu placed the purse in her hands. That same day, Yüan-wai Lu sent out servants in all directions to look for Hsiang-ling's husband and son. Soon they were found, in a village not far from Teng-chou.

A great friendship developed between the two families. Later, whenever Hsiang-ling told people the story about her purse, she would always end the tale by saying, "If you have a chance to do something good, be sure to do it. Happiness will come back to you."

Dog Steals and Rooster Crows

This story takes place more than two thousand years ago, during the period of the Warring States. Although in appearance China was still ruled by the sovereigns of the Chou Dynasty, many parts of the country had become states with their own kings. In the state of Ch'i, there lived a lord by the name of Meng Ch'ang. He was the prime minister to the king of Ch'i. He was also a very generous man. He used to invite a great number of people to live in his house, giving them food, clothes, and money to spend. These *men-k'o*, or houseguests, were mostly scholars, artists, and craftsmen, who would work for him in return. There was a time when he accommodated nearly three thousand guests in his house.

One evening, while Lord Meng Ch'ang and his guests were having dinner, a servant brought two men into the hall. One was short, skinny, and dressed in black; the other was tall, robust, and dressed in red. They bowed deeply before Lord Meng Ch'ang and said that they wanted to serve him.

"Very well," said Lord Meng Ch'ang. First he turned to the man dressed in black. "Tell me, my friend, what skills do you have? How do you earn a living?"

The man hesitated for a moment, then said in a low voice, "My lord, I bark for a living."

The guests looked at one another with puzzled expressions. Lord Meng Ch'ang thought that he had misheard. So he asked, "I am sorry, do you mean to say you bark like a dog for a living?"

"That is exactly what I mean," the man replied. "I bark just like a real dog. Bow wow!"

At this the houseguests burst into laughter. But Lord Meng Ch'ang did not laugh. Instead, he asked kindly, "My friend, tell me, how is it you bark for a living?"

"I used to be a thief," said the man. "When I found a house I wanted to break into, I would go there at night wearing a dogskin. If I was discovered, I would bark like a dog and be able to get away. That's how I used to make a living." He paused and his face grew red. "Now I know it is wrong to steal, and I promise you that I am a thief no longer."

"Good," said the lord, and then he turned to the tall man dressed in red. "My friend, what about you? How do you earn a living?"

The man smiled mischievously and said, "My lord, I crow."

Again the puzzled houseguests looked at one another.

"That is interesting," said the lord. "Tell us more."

"Every morning I used to wake up early," said the man, "and go into the courtyard and crow like a rooster. Cock-a-doodle-doo! There were always roosters in the village. And when they heard me crow, they would do the same. Cock-a-doodle-doo! We would all crow together. Thinking that it was already dawn, the people would get up. They were pleased that they had risen early, so they would pay me. That's how I used to make a living."

The houseguests roared with laughter, but Lord Meng Ch'ang only smiled. "Very well, my new friends," he said. "Welcome to my house. Sit down and dine with us."

· The houseguests were shocked. They could not believe that Lord Meng Ch'ang would take two vagabonds into his house and treat them as guests. To show their disapproval, the houseguests nicknamed the two men "Dog Steals" and "Rooster Crows."

A few months later, Lord Meng Ch'ang received a letter from the king of the state of Ch'in. The king invited Lord Meng Ch'ang to come to his country and be his prime minister. Now, Lord Meng Ch'ang knew that the king of Ch'in was a very ambitious man who acted on impulse. He didn't want to go, so he asked his king for advice.

The king of Ch'i said, "I would be sorry to lose you as my prime minister, but if you do not accept the offer, the king of Ch'in might consider this an insult and use it as an excuse to declare war against us. I think you should go."

So Lord Meng Ch'ang gathered a few of his guests, including Dog Steals and Rooster Crows, and went to the state of Ch'in. They brought with them many gifts, including a very precious white mink cloak for the king.

At first the king of Ch'in was delighted to see Lord Meng Ch'ang and the gifts he had brought, and after the lord had rested for a few days the king was ready to appoint him prime minister. But one of the king's officials, who was afraid that Lord Meng Ch'ang might become a court favorite, said to him, "I don't believe that Lord Meng Ch'ang left his king willingly to serve *Ta-wang*. I am sure he came here as a spy." The king instantly became suspicious and ordered his guards to throw Lord Meng Ch'ang into jail.

That night the houseguests who had accompanied Lord Meng Ch'ang gathered in a tavern and tried to think of a way to save him. There was one man in the group who was considered the wisest. He said, "The king of Ch'in is very fond of his youngest wife. If she puts in a word for our lord, maybe the king will let him go."

"But how can we persuade her to do so?" asked another guest. "I wish we had not given the king of Ch'in the white mink cloak. It would have been a wonderful gift for his young wife. But now it must be locked up in the treasure house. There is no way we can get it back."

While they were talking, Dog Steals quietly left the tavern. He found his way to the palace treasure house and took out a dogskin from his bosom. He pulled the skin over himself and leaped over the wall. "Bow wow!" he barked.

Two huge dogs appeared and sprang at him. "Bow wow! Bow wow!"

The three started to fight. The treasure-house guard, who had been sleeping, came out. When he saw his dogs with Dog Steals, he thought they were fighting with just another dog, so he took them into the house, tied them up, and went back to bed.

After things had quieted down, Dog Steals crept over to the treasure house and opened the door with a tool he had brought with him. There, on the top shelf of a closet, he saw the white mink cloak among the many gifts they had brought for the king and his wives. He grabbed the cloak and ran back to the tavern.

Dog Steals gave the white mink cloak to one of the houseguests, who immediately went to the palace and presented it to the king's youngest wife. She was so pleased with the gift that she agreed to talk to the king about releasing Lord Meng Ch'ang.

That night, when the king went to see her, she stopped him at the door of her chamber. "Before you come in, *Ta-wang*," she said, "I want you to grant me a wish."

"Oh, my heart and liver!" cried the king, using a Chinese expression for "sweetheart." "Haven't I given you everything you ever wanted? What is it that you want now?"

"If you don't need Lord Meng Ch'ang to be your prime minister, why not let him go home?" asked the young wife.

The king was so eager to please her that he ordered his guards to set Lord Meng Ch'ang free at once.

Lord Meng Ch'ang quickly gathered his guests at the tavern. "Let us leave before the king changes his mind. But our group is large, and if we leave together, it might arouse suspicion."

So two of the houseguests offered to stay behind and wait for a while. "We will join you at the border later," they said to Lord Meng Ch'ang.

The lord rose and headed with the rest of his group toward the border.

It was nearly midnight by the time the lord and his houseguests got there. A pale moon hung high up in the sky. Everything was quiet and the gates were locked. The sentinels who patrolled the border wall had apparently gone to bed.

"We are trapped!" cried the lord. "Nobody is allowed to go across the border at night. But we can't stay here. The king might send his guards to arrest me again."

Suddenly, they heard *clop, clop, clop,* and saw a man on a horse galloping toward them. It was one of the two houseguests who had stayed behind.

"My lord," said the man as he sprang from his horse, "after you left, an official from the palace came looking for you. He said that you had been summoned by the king. He was angry to hear that you had left and said you should not have done so without the king's permission. He went back to report to the king. I think we should cross the border before anything happens."

"What can we do?" cried the lord. "The gates won't be opened until morning."

"Let's wake up the soldiers and ask them to open the gates," suggested one guest.

"No," said the lord, "they will arrest anybody who tries to break the rules and cross the border at night."

Again, they heard *clop, clop, clop.* The other man they had left behind was galloping toward them.

"My lord," he cried as he leaped from his horse, "the king's soldiers are only five *li* away! We must cross the border at once!"

"But the gates won't be opened until morning!" cried the lord desperately.

At that moment, Rooster Crows spoke up. "Everyone, get on your horses and be ready to cross the border! The gates will be opened at once!" The next moment he had climbed up a tree and was crowing with all his might. "Cock-a-doodle-doo! Cock-a-doodle-doo!"

"What are you doing up there?" cried the lord. "You'll get us into even more trouble! Come down at once!"

But Rooster Crows kept crowing. "Cock-a-doodle-doo!"

All of a sudden, they heard an answering cock-a-doodle-doo. A rooster in the nearby village was crowing! And soon all the other roosters had

25

joined in. "Cock-a-doodle-doo! Cock-a-doodle-doo!"

The sentinels who were asleep in the fortress were awakened by the crowing. Thinking it was already morning, they jumped out of bed and ran to unlock the gates.

Lord Meng Ch'ang and his guests galloped through the gates and reached the other side of the border safely.

Early that same morning, when the king of Ch'in woke up, his young wife took out the white mink cloak and showed it to him.

"How did you get it?" asked the astonished king. He knew immediately that it was the same cloak Lord Meng Ch'ang had given him.

"I don't know," said his young wife. "One of Lord Meng Ch'ang's houseguests gave it to me as a gift."

Before the king could say anything, a soldier came to report that Lord Meng Ch'ang and his houseguests had already crossed the border. The king sighed. "The king of Ch'i is very lucky to have such a wise man as Lord Meng Ch'ang, who knows how to rally talented people around him. If I invade Ch'i, I may not win." He gave orders for his soldiers to withdraw from the border.

Back home, Lord Meng Ch'ang rewarded Dog Steals and Rooster Crows generously. He said that everyone has a talent that will prove useful one time or another.

The Two Miss Peonys

It is said that some nine hundred years ago, during the Northern Sung Dynasty, there lived a young man named Chang Chen. When Chang Chen was still a boy, he was engaged to a beautiful and wealthy girl about his own age through matchmaking. Her name was Miss Chin Peony. Unfortunately, some years later, Chang Chen's parents died and left him with very little money. Hoping to get some support, he traveled all the way to the capital, Pien-liang, where his betrothed and her parents lived.

What Chang Chen didn't know was that Miss Peony's father, Mr. Chin, a high official in the capital, was very snobbish. Mr. Chin didn't want his daughter to marry a poor man and planned to break the engagement. But since he did not have an excuse to do so, he received Chang Chen coldly and put him up in a study located in a remote corner of the garden. "You should prepare for the imperial examinations," he said. "Until you pass them and become a high official in the court, I will not allow you to marry my daughter."

Chang Chen never had a chance to see Miss Peony. He tried his best to study during the day, and often in the evening he would stand by the pond in the garden and watch a carp-fish swimming. One evening as he stood there he sighed and said, "Oh, carp-fish, how free and happy you are! And yet I know you are as lonely as I am. We have only each other for company."

Now, the carp-fish was actually a spirit. She empathized with Chang Chen and wanted to console him. So one evening, while Chang Chen was studying, she leaped out of the water, struck the ground with her tail three times, and turned herself into a girl who looked exactly like Miss Chin Peony.

The carp-fish spirit walked into Chang Chen's study and found him dozing at his desk. She took some water from his cup and sprinkled it on the young man's face.

Chang Chen woke up at once. He was surprised to see a beautiful girl in his study. "Who are you?" he asked. "Why are you here?"

"I am your betrothed, Miss Chin Peony," said the

carp-fish spirit. "I knew you were here, and wanted to visit."

Chang Chen was delighted to hear this. He quickly stood up and, making a deep bow, invited her to sit down. "I am so happy you have come. It is wonderful to finally meet you."

"I had to come at night," said the carp-fish spirit. "My father forbids me to see you. He wanted to call off our engagement, but I begged him not to. I hope you'll pass the examinations. Then my father will allow us to marry."

Chang Chen was deeply touched. "I promise you, I will try hard not to disappoint you. May I hope to see you again?"

"Tomorrow after sunset, wait for me near the pond," said the carp-fish spirit. "I will meet you there."

From then on, the two met at the pond every evening. Chang Chen never suspected that the girl was in fact a spirit.

Soon the fifteenth day of the new year arrived. It was the Yüan-hsiao Festival—the Festival of Lanterns. Miss Peony and her parents went into the garden to enjoy the evening. The carp-fish spirit, who had been waiting for Chang Chen by the pond, quickly hid herself behind a willow tree, for fear of being caught as an impostor. Chang Chen, arriving there a few minutes late, saw Miss Peony and went over to talk to her.

Now, Miss Peony had never met Chang Chen before. When she saw him, she began to scream: "Bandit, bandit, help, help!"

Her father was furious when he saw Chang Chen. "How dare you approach my daughter," he blasted. "Get out of here!" He ordered his servants to throw Chang Chen out of the garden.

Chang Chen was deeply hurt. The carp-fish spirit caught up with him outside the estate and began to walk with him. But Chang Chen thought she was the girl who had called him a bandit, and he refused to talk to her.

"I had to pretend that I didn't know you," explained the carp-fish spirit, "otherwise my father would have punished me for talking to you. I think the best thing for us to do is to leave this place and get married."

"I am very poor," said Chang Chen. "If you marry me, you will have to live a hard life."

"I have some money with me," said the carp-fish spirit. "Besides, we can always find ways to make a living. Don't you worry."

Chang Chen finally believed the girl was telling him the truth and agreed to do as she had suggested. The two decided to leave the capital at once.

As they walked through the streets, they found that

the Yüan-hsiao festivities had already begun. Firecrackers were going off everywhere. The streets were crowded. A parade of colorful lanterns resembling different kinds of animals and historical figures moved on as the crowds watched and cheered.

Unfortunately for the young lovers, Miss Peony's father, Mr. Chin, together with several other high officials, had come to watch the celebration. From the platform on which he was standing, he saw Chang Chen and the carp-fish spirit in the crowd. Thinking his daughter had run away with Chang Chen, Mr. Chin flew into a rage. His guards were ordered to arrest the couple and take them back to his house.

The moment Mr. Chin returned home he began to yell at his wife: "How dare you let our daughter run away with this penniless man and disgrace us!"

"*Lao-yeh*, you are wrong," said his wife. "Our daughter never set foot out of the house. She is in her chamber. I can get her right away."

Mr. Chin's eyes were as large as walnuts when he saw his daughter appear in the doorway with his wife. "Then who was the girl we caught running away with Chang Chen? Bring them both in!" he commanded his guards.

Mr. Chin could not believe his eyes. In front of him stood two Miss Peonys!

The real Miss Peony was very angry. "Who are

you?" she said to the carp-fish spirit. "How dare you impersonate me!"

The carp-fish spirit realized that she had to go along with the story she had made up for Chang Chen, so she said, "I *am* Miss Peony. You are the impostor!"

The two began to quarrel, each accusing the other of being the impostor. Mr. Chin was totally confused. He finally decided to contact Pao Kung, the imperial investigator, for help.

When the carp-fish spirit heard this, she began to worry. Since Pao Kung had the power to expel demons and spirits, she would be forced to reveal her identity.

Late at night, when nobody was watching, the carp-fish spirit hurried back to the pond. "Tortoise spirit!" she called. "I am in great danger!"

The tortoise spirit emerged from the water. "What is it, my dear carp-fish? What's wrong?"

"Mr. Chin has sent for Pao Kung. If he comes tomorrow, he will force me to reveal my true identity. I will then have to leave Chang Chen."

"Don't you worry," said the tortoise spirit. "I will deal with Pao Kung."

The next morning, the tortoise spirit turned himself into Pao Kung, changed his little shrimp and crab friends into guards, and formed an instant procession. They went out through the back entrance of the garden and onto the road. Having gone a distance, they turned

around and marched back toward the mansion. Just before they reached it, the tortoise-spirit Pao Kung saw the real Pao Kung and his guards coming from the opposite direction.

Mr. Chin was flabbergasted when he saw the two processions—two Pao Kungs, each escorted by their guards. "Oh, what am I going to do?" he cried. But he had to allow them both into his house, since he could not determine who was truly Pao Kung.

The real Pao Kung was outraged to see someone impersonating him. He ordered his guards to bring him his sword, which had the supernatural power to expose the original shapes of spirits.

"Wait," cried the tortoise spirit as the real Pao Kung raised his sword. "Pao Kung is wise and just. If you are the real Pao Kung, try to solve this case with fairness. If you cannot, you are no Pao Kung."

Pao Kung agreed and put down his sword. Two temporary courts were set up in the hall. The real Pao Kung sat at a desk on the left side; the tortoise-spirit Pao Kung sat at a desk on the right side.

"Open court!" said the real Pao Kung.

"Open court!" imitated the tortoise spirit.

"*Ouh! . . . Ouh! . . . Ouh!*" cried the guards of the real Pao Kung.

"*Ouh! . . . Ouh! . . . Ouh!*" imitated the shrimp and crab soldiers with delight.

The two Pao Kungs ordered the two Miss Peonys and Chang Chen to be brought in.

Still quarreling with each other, the girls entered. Then they took turns telling their stories. Each insisted that she was the real Miss Peony who had lived in her father's house all her life.

The real Pao Kung was soon convinced which of the two was the real Miss Peony, but he sympathized with the carp-fish spirit and admired her for her love for Chang Chen. He decided not to reveal her identity, because he knew that it would mean an end to her relationship with the young man.

Shaking his head and pretending that he could not tell the difference, he said, "I cannot solve this case. It is giving me a headache. I am going home." He rose and left with his guards.

The tortoise-spirit Pao Kung, laughing to himself, also left with his shrimp and crab soldiers.

Mr. Chin was very upset. "I am going to appeal to the Jade Emperor and request that he send Chang T'ien-shih, the Sorcerer from Heaven, to expel the evil spirit."

The carp-fish spirit knew that Chang T'ien-shih was merciless, so she decided to tell Chang Chen the truth. Taking him aside, she said, "I am only a carp-fish spirit. I love you and impersonated your betrothed. Now I must go."

"Let's go together," said Chang Chen. "I don't love

Miss Peony. All she cares about is herself. I want to marry you."

So the two walked out of Mr. Chin's house together.

Suddenly, they heard a voice from the sky. It was Chang T'ien-shih standing on a cloud flying toward them.

"Stop," cried Chang T'ien-shih. "I have come to conquer the evil spirit that dares to create chaos on the earth!"

The two lovers ran as fast as they could, but Chang T'ien-shih was quicker.

Finally, the carp-fish spirit gave up hope. She threw herself on the ground and began to weep. Just then she heard a gentle voice calling her.

"Carp-fish spirit! Carp-fish spirit!"

When she looked up, she saw Kuan-yin, the Buddha of Compassion, standing before her. "Oh, Kuan-yin," she cried, "please save me."

"Carp-fish spirit, listen to me," said Kuan-yin, as she motioned Chang T'ien-shih to withdraw. "The world is full of sorrow. A spirit is not allowed to mix with human beings. Come with me and nurture yourself with prayers and fasting, and you will become an immortal someday."

"No," said the carp-fish spirit. "I love Chang Chen. I want to marry him. Please make me a real woman instead."

"Are you willing to give up your supernatural power?" asked Kuan-yin.

"Yes, as long as I can marry Chang Chen," said the carp-fish spirit.

"Think again," said Kuan-yin. "You have nurtured your supernatural spirit for almost a thousand years, and you will soon become immortal. If you give up your power, you will only live a human life. You might regret your decision."

"No," said the carp-fish spirit. "I will never regret it."

"Very well," said Kuan-yin. "I will pluck out your three magic scales, and then you will become an ordinary woman. I'm afraid it is going to hurt a great deal." She waved her hand, and the spirit turned back into a carp-fish.

The carp-fish spirit felt terrible pain as Kuan-yin plucked out her three magic scales. She somersaulted three times. Immediately, all her supernatural power left her, and she became a real woman, far more beautiful than Miss Peony.

She ran back to the pond to say goodbye to her friends and then followed Chang Chen back to his hometown. They started to build a happy life, and when they got married, all the shrimps, fish, and tortoises from the pond, as well as those from the lakes and seas, attended the wedding.

The Ho-shih Jade

During the period of the Warring States, the kings of China made war on one another, fighting for power and land. When tired of fighting, they would send envoys to negotiate a settlement. These negotiations were sometimes called tongue wars. At one time, there were seven states: Ch'in, Ch'u, Ch'i, Yen, Han, Wei, and Chao. Ch'in was the strongest, while Chao was the weakest.

The king of Chao had a chamberlain named Miao Hsien. One day Miao Hsien bought a jadestone from a stranger for five hundred *liang* of gold. When he asked a jade expert to appraise it, he was told that it was the famous Ho-shih Jade, named after Pien Ho, the man who discovered it. This jade was the rarest kind of precious stone in the world. In the dark, it was luminous; indoors, it would keep a room warm in winter and cool in summer and repel insects. The jade expert advised Miao Hsien to keep the jade in a safe place so that it would not be stolen.

The king of Chao somehow heard about the jade and asked Miao Hsien to show it to him. Miao Hsien feared that once the king saw the jade he would want it, so he planned to take the jade and run away. But one of Miao Hsien's houseguests, a man named Lin Hsiang-ju, advised him not to do so, saying that he would be asking for trouble. He persuaded Miao Hsien to offer the jade to the king as a national treasure.

Miao Hsien followed this advice; the king was delighted and promoted Miao Hsien to a very high position. Miao Hsien then realized that Lin Hsiang-ju had been very wise, so he entrusted him with other important matters.

Some time later, when the jade expert went to the state of Ch'in to set some jadestones, he told the king of Ch'in about the Ho-shih Jade and its unique features. The king of Ch'in, who was a very ambitious and greedy man, wanted the jade for himself. He gathered his officials and asked them how he could take the jade away from the state of Chao. His uncle and prime minister, Wei Jan, suggested that he offer fifteen cities in the Yu-yang area in exchange for the jade.

"What?" cried the king of Ch'in. "Is such a jade worth fifteen cities? Only a fool would do that."

"We would not be making the offer in earnest," said Wei Jan. "The king of Chao has always been afraid of us, because he fears that we are going to invade his state. Therefore, if we offer to exchange fifteen cities for the jade, he would not dare refuse. Once the jade is here, we can keep it. We will not give him the fifteen cities. Would he dare to ask for them?"

The king of Ch'in thought this was a good idea, so he sent an envoy to the king of Chao with a letter offering fifteen cities in the Yu-yang area for the jade.

As expected, this offer worried the king of Chao. He knew that if he sent the jade to the king of Ch'in he would not get the fifteen cities in return, and yet he did not dare refuse the offer, for fear that the king of Ch'in would declare war on the state of Chao. So he summoned his high officials to court.

The high officials offered all kinds of advice, but they could not agree on anything. One official then suggested that the king send a wise and brave man to the state of Ch'in as his envoy. If the king of Ch'in really signed over the deeds of the fifteen cities to Chao, the envoy should leave the jade there. If not, he should bring the jade back.

The king of Chao liked the idea, but he didn't know whom to send. He looked from one official to another, but they all lowered their heads and did not say a word.

Then Miao Hsien stepped forward and said, "I have a houseguest, Lin Hsiang-ju. He is both wise and brave. If *Ta-wang* appoints him envoy, I am sure he will be able to accomplish the task successfully."

So the king of Chao summoned Lin Hsiang-ju to the palace. He was delighted to find Lin Hsiang-ju an unusually intelligent man, but to make sure that he was capable of undertaking the task, the king asked, "The king of Ch'in has offered to exchange fifteen cities for the Ho-shih Jade; do you think that I should accept his offer?"

"Ch'in is strong and Chao is weak," said Lin Hsiang-ju. "It would not be wise for *Ta-wang* to turn down the offer."

"If the king of Ch'in takes the jade but does not give us the cities, what should we do?" asked the king of Chao, testing him further.

"The king of Ch'in is offering a high price for the jade," said Lin Hsiang-ju. "If we do not accept the offer, it will make us look very bad. If we present the jade to the king of Ch'in before he gives us fifteen cities, it will show that we are sincere and courteous. If the king of Ch'in denies us the fifteen cities when he has the jade in his hand, he will be in the wrong!" Lin Hsiang-ju paused, waiting to see the king's reaction.

"I plan to send an envoy to the state of Ch'in with the jade. Whom do you think I should send?" asked the king of Chao.

"I would be honored to go. If the king of Ch'in signs over to us the fifteen cities, I will leave the jade with him. Otherwise, your lowly servant will bring the jade safely back to *Ta-wang*," Lin Hsiang-ju replied with confidence.

The king of Chao was pleased and appointed Lin Hsiang-ju his envoy. Lin Hsiang-ju then laid out his plan in detail.

After several days of preparation, including a five-day fast and a solemn farewell ceremony, Lin Hsiang-ju took the Ho-shih Jade and set out for Hsien-yang, the capital of Ch'in, accompanied only by a guard.

When the king of Ch'in heard that the envoy from Chao was coming with the jade, he was overjoyed. Seated on his throne and flanked by his officials, he summoned Lin Hsiang-ju to the palace as soon as he arrived.

With his head bowed, Lin Hsiang-ju approached the throne carrying a box that held the jade. He opened the box, took out the silk pouch that protected the jade, and offered it to the king of Ch'in.

The king opened the pouch and carefully removed its contents. Immaculate, the stone gleamed in his hands. It was truly a rare treasure. After examining the jade, the king passed it on to his officials, who immediately congratulated him for securing such a priceless gem. They shouted, "May *Ta-wang* live ten thousand years!"

The king of Ch'in then ordered his servant to take the jade to his wives and concubines and show it to them. Lin Hsiang-ju waited for a long time, but the jade was not returned to the king's table.

Seeing that the king mentioned nothing about the fifteen cities, Lin Hsiang-ju said, "There is a flaw in the jade. Please allow me to show it to *Ta-wang*."

The king quickly ordered his servant to bring the jade back to Lin Hsiang-ju. Once the jade was in Lin Hsiang-ju's hands, he took several steps backward until he was very close to a pillar. Then he said angrily to the king, "This jade is one of the most precious treasures in the world. *Ta-wang* wrote to the king of Chao offering fifteen cities for the jade. His Majesty discussed the proposal with his officials, who felt it might be a ploy and tried to dissuade him from accepting the offer. But I argued that because *Ta-wang* is such a powerful king, there is no reason to doubt his sincerity. My king followed my advice and sent me here with the jade. This shows how sincere he is. On the other hand, when *Ta-wang* took the jade from my hands, he did not even rise from his throne. Then *Ta-wang* showed the jade not only to his subjects but also to his wives and con-

cubines. This is an insult to the precious jade. In addition, *Ta-wang* never mentioned the fifteen cities he had previously promised. It proves that *Ta-wang* has no real intention of exchanging fifteen cities for the jade. I am going to take the jade back to my king."

The bold Lin Hsiang-ju then pointed to the pillar. "If *Ta-wang* tries to take the jade from me by force, I will smash it and then my head on this pillar. We will both be destroyed, but *Ta-wang* will not get the jade either!" He raised the jade as if ready to carry out his threat.

"Don't do it!" cried the king of Ch'in. "I won't fail your king." He ordered one of his officials to bring a map. The map was placed on the table, and the king of Ch'in pointed out fifteen cities to Lin Hsiang-ju.

Suspecting the king of playing another trick, Lin Hsiang-ju said to him, "In order to please *Ta-wang*, His Majesty the king of Chao was willing to relinquish the jade. Before I left, he fasted for five days and summoned all his officials to see the jade off in a solemn ceremony. *Ta-wang* should follow his example: fast for five days, and receive the jade in a ceremony where envoys from other states are present. If *Ta-wang* refuses, I would rather die than turn over the jade to *Ta-wang*."

Seeing how determined Lin Hsiang-ju was, the king of Ch'in thought that it would be best to go along with his demands. He ordered a fast for five days and sent Lin Hsiang-ju back to his lodgings.

But Lin Hsiang-ju was afraid that the king of Ch'in might still have other tricks to play, so he ordered his guard to disguise himself as a poor man, tie the bag that contained the jade around his waist, and return to Chao. He also wrote a letter to the king of Chao saying that he was sending his guard back with the jade, while he himself was staying behind to deal with the king of Ch'in.

The king of Ch'in did not fast at all. He ordered his servants to decorate the palace and prepare many expensive gifts. Envoys from every state were invited to witness the ceremony.

When they had all arrived, the king of Ch'in summoned his official of protocol to escort Lin Hsiang-ju to the throne room. Lin Hsiang-ju walked up to the king and bowed. Seeing that Lin Hsiang-ju was empty-handed, the king said, "I have fasted for five days and am ready to receive the jade—where is it?"

Lin Hsiang-ju replied, "Since King Mu's reign, there have been twenty kings in the state of Ch'in, and all were treacherous and dishonest. *Ta-wang* has a similar reputation. For fear of being cheated and unable to fulfill my king's task, I ordered my guard to take the jade back to my king. For this I deserve death; please do with me whatever *Ta-wang* pleases." He bent his head and waited.

The king of Ch'in was furious. "You blamed me for not showing enough respect for the jade. I followed your advice and met your demands. And yet you sent the jade back to Chao. You have cheated me! I am going to kill you!" He ordered his guards to bind Lin Hsiang-ju with ropes.

Lin Hsiang-ju did not resist. "*Ta-wang* should listen to what I have to say; if my words do not satisfy him, it will not be too late to kill me."

"Speak!" said the king of Ch'in impatiently.

"Ch'in is strong and Chao is weak. The state of Chao cannot afford to make an enemy of the state of Ch'in. If *Ta-wang* really wants to exchange fifteen cities for the jade, why not send an envoy with me to Chao with the deed to the cities? When our king has the deed in his hands, he would not dare to keep the jade from *Ta-wang*. I know that I have offended *Ta-wang* and deserve death, so I have already informed my king that I may not return alive. *Ta-wang* might as well throw me into a caldron of boiling oil, so that all the kings will know that *Ta-wang* killed the envoy of Chao in his effort to possess the Ho-shih Jade. Let them decide who is right and who is wrong."

The king of Ch'in and his officials looked at one

49

another without a word. All the envoys from the other states knew how cruel a man the king of Ch'in was, and feared for Lin Hsiang-ju's life.

Wei Jan, the king's uncle, quickly walked up to his nephew and whispered in his ear, "I don't think it is wise to kill Lin Hsiang-ju now. It will not only ruin our reputation but also make the state of Chao our enemy. It would be better to let him go."

The king nodded his head. As the soldiers started to take Lin Hsiang-ju away, the king began to laugh. "Wait!" he said as he turned to Lin Hsiang-ju. "I was only testing your courage. I wanted to see what kind of person you really are and how you would react in the face of death. It seems to me now that you are really a brave man. The king of Chao is lucky to have you as his envoy. No, I am not going to kill you."

So instead of executing Lin Hsiang-ju, the king entertained him with a banquet and sent him back home. The king of Chao was so pleased with Lin Hsiang-ju's courage and ingenuity that he appointed him one of his highest-ranking officials.

The king of Ch'in never gave the king of Chao the fifteen cities he had promised. So, of course, he never got the jade.

The Prime Minister
and the General

Several months after Lin Hsiang-ju had returned to
the state of Chao, the king of Ch'in sent an envoy to
invite the king of Chao to meet him at a city called
Mien-ch'ih. The king of Chao became worried again.
He knew the king of Ch'in had one time played a
similar trick on the king of Ch'u and made him a pris-
oner. The king was not sure that such a trip was safe.

But General Lien P'o and Lin Hsiang-ju, who had
now become an official in the king's court, both
thought that if their king did not accept the invitation
it would show that he was a coward and would make
Chao look very weak. So Lin Hsiang-ju asked to accompany the king to Mien-ch'ih, and have the troops
commanded by General Lien P'o follow at a distance.

As General Lien P'o stood by the side of the road

seeing the king off, he said, "*Ch'en* cannot predict what is going to happen on this trip. If *Ta-wang* does not return to Chao in thirty days, please allow *Ch'en* and the high officials of the court to support *T'ai-tzu*'s ascension to the throne, so that the king of Ch'in will gain nothing from the state of Chao by detaining *Ta-wang*."

The king agreed and proceeded toward Mien-ch'ih.

When the king of Chao arrived in Mien-ch'ih, the king of Ch'in greeted him in a solemn ceremony. A banquet was held in his honor. In the middle of the meal, the king of Ch'in said to his guest, "I heard that you are a very good musician. I have a *se*. Would you mind playing it for me?"

The king of Chao's face reddened at this insult, but he dared not refuse. The king of Ch'in ordered one of his servants to bring in the *se*—a stringed wooden instrument—and place it on the table in front of the king of Chao. Reluctantly, the king of Chao played a tune.

"Excellent," said the king of Ch'in, laughing. "Official of historical records, write this down in our book: On this very day, the king of Chao has played the *se* to amuse the king of Ch'in."

Lin Hsiang-ju quickly walked up to the king of Ch'in. "My king has learned that *Ta-wang* is good at percussion instruments. Here, I have a wine jar. Would

Ta-wang please play it?" With the wine jar in his hand, he knelt down in front of the king of Ch'in.

The king of Ch'in looked angry. He said nothing and refused to play.

"*Ta-wang* thinks that he is powerful," said Lin Hsiang-ju, holding up the wine jar as if he was about to strike the king's head with it. "However, since I am within such a short distance, I can easily make you play. If any of your soldiers tries to kill me, my blood will splash upon you." He fixed his eyes on the king of Ch'in.

The king of Ch'in was stunned. The blood of a man on him could become a deadly curse, and he did not want that! The officials of Ch'in began to reprimand Lin Hsiang-ju. Some wanted to have him arrested. But Lin Hsiang-ju stood firm and would not budge.

Finally, the king of Ch'in gave in. He beat the wine jar several times and made some noise.

Lin Hsiang-ju rose to his feet and called the official of historical records. "Record these words in our book: On this very date, the king of Ch'in beat a wine jar to entertain the king of Chao."

At this point, several officials of the state of Ch'in, who had received instructions from their king before the meeting, walked over to the king of Chao and said, "Please give the king of Ch'in fifteen cities to celebrate his birthday."

Lin Hsiang-ju immediately said to the king of Ch'in, "If *Ta-wang* wants fifteen cities from Chao, the king of Chao should also get something in return. What about giving him Hsien-yang as a gift?" Hsien-yang was the capital of Ch'in.

The king of Ch'in knew that he could not afford to lose his capital, so he decided to make peace. He said, "The king of Chao and I are friends. Please do not say anything more."

As the meeting drew to a close, some of his officials suggested that the king of Ch'in have the king of Chao and Lin Hsiang-ju detained. But when the king of Ch'in learned that General Lien P'o's troops were stationed not far away and could attack his state at any time, he decided not to follow his officials' advice. On the contrary, he began to respect the king of Chao, and proposed that the two become sworn allies. He promised that he would never invade Chao, and, to show his sincerity, he even sent his son to Chao as a hostage. So the meeting at Mien-ch'ih ended without any incident, and the king of Chao returned to his state safely with Lin Hsiang-ju.

Impressed by Lin Hsiang-ju's wisdom and bravery, the king of Chao appointed him prime minister. But General Lien P'o became very angry when he learned that Lin Hsiang-ju had become his superior. He said to his officers, "I have fought and won many battles so that the state of Chao can be as safe as it is now. And yet Lin Hsiang-ju is the one who gets the credit. He did nothing but talk. It is not fair that he should have a higher position than mine. He rose from a very low social status. If I see him on the streets, I will kill him."

Lien P'o's words reached Lin Hsiang-ju's ears. The prime minister became sad and worried, because he knew that conflict between him and the general would endanger the state of Chao. So he often used illness as an excuse to stay away from court meetings, and he avoided direct contact with Lien P'o.

Lin Hsiang-ju's houseguests were concerned about his safety, but they did not know what to do. One day, when Lin Hsiang-ju was riding in a carriage, he was told that Lien P'o's carriage was coming toward him. He quickly ordered his driver to pull over to the side of the road and let Lien P'o's carriage pass.

When Lin Hsiang-ju's houseguests heard about this incident, they became very angry and said to him, "We left our homes and came to serve you because we thought you were a brave and noble man. But now you seem to be afraid of General Lien P'o, even though your position is higher than his. When he threatened you, you never fought back. Instead, you avoided him by not attending court meetings, and went as far as making way for him on the roads. We did not know that you were such a coward! We are ashamed and feel that we are inferior to others. That is why we have come to bid you farewell." They bowed and were about to leave.

Lin Hsiang-ju quickly stopped them. "Please do not misunderstand me. I am not the coward you think." He invited them to sit down and began to explain. "I avoided meeting with General Lien P'o not because I am afraid of him. There is a very important reason."

"What is it?" asked his houseguests.

"Tell me," said Lin Hsiang-ju, "who is more formidable: the king of Ch'in or General Lien P'o?"

"The king of Ch'in, of course," answered his houseguests without hesitation.

"That's right. If you remember how I defeated the king's attempts to seize the Ho-shih Jade and to humiliate our king at Mien-ch'ih, you should know that I was not intimidated by the king of Ch'in at all. If I am not afraid of the king of Ch'in, how can I be afraid of General Lien P'o? The reason why the king of Ch'in dares not invade our state is because he knows that General Lien P'o and I are united in serving our king. If we were fighting each other, one of us would be destroyed. It would give the king of Ch'in the opportunity to invade. With this in mind, I have avoided any confrontation with General Lien P'o. I am concerned

about the safety of our state, not about which official should rank first."

Lin Hsiang-ju's houseguests were deeply touched by his words and took them to heart. One day, when they were drinking in a wine shop, a few of Lien P'o's followers came in. They began to pick a quarrel with Lin Hsiang-ju's houseguests over the seats. But the houseguests remembered their patron's example. They quickly rose and left the seats to Lien P'o's followers.

Lien P'o became more and more arrogant. Seeing that Lin Hsiang-ju no longer attended court meetings, he began to believe that his rival really was afraid of him.

Then a wise man named Yü Ch'ing traveled to Chao and learned about the feud between Lin Hsiang-ju and Lien P'o. He went to visit the king of Chao.

"The most important officials in *Ta-wang*'s court are Prime Minister Lin and General Lien. Is that right?" asked Yü Ch'ing.

"Yes, of course," the king of Chao replied.

"In the past, all the important officials of the court were noble-minded and cooperated with one another. But *Ta-wang*'s two officials are like fire and water, unable to stand each other's presence. This is very dangerous for the state of Chao. Would *Ta-wang* like me to be a peacemaker between the two?"

The king of Chao agreed and authorized Yü Ch'ing to go ahead.

When Yü Ch'ing visited Lien P'o, he first praised the general for his merits. Lien P'o was delighted. Then Yü Ch'ing said, "According to the war merits, General, you rank first. As to nobility, Prime Minister Lin is first."

Lien P'o immediately became upset. "Lin Hsiang-ju is a coward. He has nothing but a quick tongue. Why do you say that he is noble?"

Yü Ch'ing smiled and replied, "Lin Hsiang-ju is not a coward. He is a man with a broad vision and never shows off. Before coming here, I talked to several of his houseguests, and they told me that the reason Lin Hsiang-ju avoids any conflict with you is because he believes it would weaken the state of Chao. He cares more about his country than about his pride."

Lien P'o suddenly understood. He felt very much ashamed and said to Yü Ch'ing, "If you had not pointed this out to me, I would not have seen my mistake. It does seem that I am not as noble as Prime Minister Lin." He then asked Yü Ch'ing to inform Lin Hsiang-ju that he was on his way to the prime minister's residence to apologize.

Lien P'o followed the tradition of that time and dressed himself like a public penitent. He bared his shoulders and tied a piece of firewood to his back. Then he walked up the steps that led to Lin Hsiang-ju's house and knelt down at the entrance to the hall.

When Lin Hsiang-ju, who was working in his study, learned from Yü Ch'ing that Lien P'o was at the door, he rushed out to greet him. Realizing that he was wearing only his short robe, he hurried back and grabbed his long one. Throwing the robe over his shoulders, he ran to the entrance.

"General Lien P'o," he cried as he knelt down facing the general, "why are you doing this?"

"I was blind enough not to see that *Ch'eng-shiang* was tolerating me for the sake of our country," said Lien P'o as tears rolled down his cheeks. "I deeply regret my shameful behavior and have come to ask for *Ch'eng-shiang*'s forgiveness. Please punish me in any way you like."

"Please do not say this," said Lin Hsiang-ju as he wiped the general's tears with his sleeve. "I am from the younger generation and need your guidance in many ways." He quickly helped Lien P'o to his feet. "We two are responsible for our country's security, and must answer to our king. We should be united in dealing with our enemies. Please forgive me for my faults."

Lin Hsiang-ju unfastened the firewood that was tied

to Lien P'o's back and threw it aside. Then he took off his long robe and helped Lien P'o put it on. The two went into the hall together, where tea was served.

Lien P'o suggested that they be *sheng-ssu-chih-chiao* —life-and-death friends. Lin Hsiang-ju immediately agreed. They went down on their knees and swore never to betray each other.

From that time on, Lin Hsiang-ju and Lien P'o always got along. Chao became safe, prosperous, and strong for many years.

The king of Chao was very pleased that the discord was resolved between his two most important officials. He rewarded the wise man Yü Ch'ing with a hundred *liang* of gold and appointed him a high official of his court.

The Clever Magistrate

One cold winter day, a farmer was carrying two buckets of spoiled food from a restaurant to his pigsty. As he was passing a coat shop, he accidentally spilled some of the slop on the ground. Sour cabbage, rotten eggs, and fish bones scattered all over the ground. Ugh! Ugh! What a smell!

The shopkeeper, who happened to be standing inside the door, saw this and was furious. He rushed out, grabbed the man, and shouted, "You dirty beggar! Look what you've done in front of my shop! It will be impossible to get rid of the smell! How are you going to pay for the damage?"

"I am so sorry," said the farmer. "I will clean it up right away. As for the damage, all I have is this coin."

He took out a coin and handed it to the shopkeeper.

The shopkeeper snatched the coin, put it between his teeth, and bit down on it. The metal was soft, which proved that it contained silver. He thrust it into his pocket and said, "All right, I will take it. But you still need to clean up the mess."

"Let me go and get some rags and a mop," said the farmer. "I will be right back."

"No," said the shopkeeper. "I want you to clean it up right away. It smells so bad that I am going to be sick. Take off your coat and wipe up the mess."

"Please don't ask me to do that!" cried the farmer. "This is the only quilted coat I have, and if I use it to wipe up the mess, it will be ruined. I won't be able to wear it anymore."

"That's your problem, not mine!" said the shop-keeper. "In fact, the coat you are wearing is no better than rags. If you don't do what I say, I am going to take you to court."

The farmer pleaded with him to reconsider, but the shopkeeper would not relent.

Just then they heard, "Make way for the magistrate! Make way for the magistrate!"

The county magistrate was coming down the road in his sedan chair. When he saw the commotion, he ordered his guards to put down the chair and bring the two men before him.

"What is the matter?" he asked.

The shopkeeper quickly replied, "*Ta-jen*, this man made a mess in front of my shop. He gave me a coin to pay for the damage, but when I asked him to wipe up the mess, he wouldn't do it."

The magistrate stepped down from his chair and went over to look at the mess. Sour cabbage, rotten eggs, and fish bones were scattered all over the place. Ugh! Ugh! What a smell!

"Why don't you clean up the mess?" asked the magistrate.

"He wants me to wipe up the mess with my coat," said the farmer. "It will be ruined if I do so. And this is the only coat I have."

"Is that what you want?" the magistrate asked the shopkeeper.

"Yes, that is exactly what I want."

"And you will not settle for less?"

"No, I will not settle for anything less."

"Well," said the magistrate to the farmer, "if that is what he wants, you'd better do it."

"*Ta-jen*, have mercy! I can't do that!" cried the farmer. "Without the coat I will freeze to death."

"I am sorry," said the magistrate. "But that doesn't change anything. If you don't do it, I will have to put you in jail."

"That is not just!" cried the farmer.

"Hmm . . ." said the magistrate. He looked angry.

"*Ouh! Ouh! Ouh!*" cried the guards. "*Ouh! Ouh! Ouh!*" They looked threatening.

The farmer realized that there was no way out. Reluctantly, he used his coat to clean up the mess. Sour cabbage, rotten eggs, and fish bones. Ugh! Ugh! What a smell! He threw the coat into one of his buckets and stood shivering in front of the magistrate.

The shopkeeper laughed. "Ha, ha, ha!"

"Well," said the magistrate to the shopkeeper, "are you satisfied now?"

"Yes, *Ta-jen*, I am completely satisfied."

"No more complaints?"

"No more complaints!" said the shopkeeper.

"Case closed," said the magistrate.

"Case closed."

"But his case against you is now open."

"What!" said the shopkeeper, stunned.

"Well, you see, he is now freezing without a coat. In such weather he could catch a cold. Is that not possible?" asked the magistrate.

"Yes, *Ta-jen*."

"His cold could develop into pneumonia. Is that not possible?"

"Yes, *Ta-jen*."

"Then he could die. His family could sue you for

murder, and if you are convicted, you would be put to death. Isn't that almost inevitable?"

"Yes, *Ta-jen*."

"Well, I don't think you can afford that, can you?"

"Oh, no, *Ta-jen*. I cannot afford that. What shall I do?"

"Well, it would be better to settle this out of court."

"Yes, yes, we'd better settle this out of court. But how?"

"We should get him a coat so he won't catch a cold."

"But where can we get one?"

"Right here, from your coat shop."

The shopkeeper looked as if he had swallowed a fly alive. He yelled at the farmer, "Go get a coat and be gone!"

The farmer went into the shop, picked out a very cheap coat, and came out. The magistrate stopped him.

"You poor thing!" he said. "Look at the coat you've got. It is so thin. You could still catch a cold, isn't that so?"

"Yes, *Ta-jen*."

"You might get pneumonia, isn't that so?"

"Yes, *Ta-jen*."

"You might even die, isn't that so?"

"Yes, *Ta-jen*."

"And then your family could come and harass this nice gentleman. I know all your tricks!" The magistrate turned to one of his guards. "Go into the shop and get him the warmest coat you can find."

So the guard went into the shop and picked out the warmest coat he could find for the farmer. As you might guess, the warmest coat happened to be the most expensive.

When the farmer left, the magistrate smiled at the shopkeeper. "Well, what do you think about the way I settled this case? Didn't I handle it very well?"

"Yes, *Ta-jen*," the shopkeeper said glumly. "There is no question about that."

"I am glad I was able to take care of this case," said the magistrate. "You have to watch out for these troublemakers. Next time, if you have a case like this, don't try to settle it yourself. Be sure to let me handle it for you."

Mr. Yeh's New Year

Some six hundred years ago, on New Year's Eve, Mr. Yeh was on his way home after being gone for almost a year. In his sack was a silver *yüan-pao*, the salary for a year's teaching in a private school some seventy *li* away. Mr. Yeh was very happy. He knew his wife would be waiting for him and for the money as well. She needed the money to buy food and wine for the New Year's Eve dinner.

No Chinese could afford to miss New Year's Eve dinner. It was the most important meal of the year, even more important than the dinner on New Year's Day. The Chinese always believed that a well-provided New Year's Eve dinner would usher them smoothly into a prosperous new year.

A typical New Year's Eve feast would include *ssu-ch'üan*, or four "wholes"—a whole chicken, a whole duck, a whole fish, and a whole leg of pork; four kinds of cold meat; *pa-pao-fan*, or "eight-treasure rice," a sweet rice dish with eight ingredients; and *pa-pao-ts'ai*, the "eight valuables," which is made of eight different kinds of vegetables and soybeans. If people could afford it, they would cook enough to last for the fifteen days of the New Year celebration. It not only showed that they were well-off enough to have food left over from the previous year, it also let them enjoy visiting with relatives and friends during the holidays without having to worry about cooking.

Mr. Yeh was quite sure that his wife had used up every penny she had and was "waiting for rice to put into the pot," as the saying goes. He wished he had wings so he could fly back home and give that silver *yüan-pao* to his wife right away. As he walked on, he started to plan the menu for the New Year's Eve dinner. He knew that they would probably not be able to buy four "wholes." But at least his wife could get some pork and cook his favorite, *hung-shao-jou*—pork stewed with red wine and red soybean sauce—which he would definitely wash down with his favorite rice wine . . .

What happened in the next few seconds was almost too sudden to describe. Mr. Yeh saw a woman run toward the river, just about to throw herself in. It was

A-ken Sao, he realized, the wife of carpenter A-ken. He rushed to stop her, and in a flash A-ken Sao was caught in his arms.

"Let me go!" she cried. "Let me go!"

But Mr. Yeh would not let go. "A-ken Sao!" he said. "You mustn't end your life like this! What is the matter?"

"Let me die!" cried A-ken Sao. "I have not heard from A-ken for a whole year. He has either died or abandoned me. The rent on our land is long overdue, and now the landlord wants to sell my daughter, Ying-hua. I don't know what to do."

"Don't worry," said Mr. Yeh. "I am sure A-ken has just been delayed."

"It can't be true. Since he left home a year ago, he has not written or even sent a message to me. I know he is dead! Oh, let me die!" cried A-ken Sao. But the more she struggled, the tighter Mr. Yeh held on.

"I am certain A-ken did write," said Mr. Yeh. He was thinking hard for words.

Suddenly A-ken Sao stopped struggling. "So you have a letter for me?"

Mr. Yeh let go of her and pretended to search his pockets. Then he smiled apologetically. "No, I don't have a letter."

"Oh!" cried A-ken Sao. She started for the river again.

"Don't, don't!" said Mr. Yeh. "A-ken didn't ask me to bring you a letter, but he sent you some money." He took out the precious silver *yüan-pao*, rubbed it carefully on his robe, and handed it to A-ken Sao.

A-ken Sao broke into a big smile as she took the *yüan-pao*. "Ying-hua is saved! Buddha protects us! Thank you, Mr. Yeh."

Mr. Yeh watched A-ken Sao hurry away. "There goes my New Year's Eve dinner!" he mumbled to himself. With heavy steps, he walked slowly toward home.

Sure enough, Mrs. Yeh was standing by the door when he arrived. "Old man, here you are! I was worried that something might have happened. You must be tired. I'll get you some water to wash your face."

After Mr. Yeh had washed his face and sat down at the table, Mrs. Yeh said, "Old man, was this a good year for you?"

"Oh, it was a good year. I earned a silver *yüan-pao*."

"Thanks be to Buddha! Now we can have a decent New Year's Eve dinner. Where is it?"

"Old woman, I don't have it anymore."

"What! What did you do with it?"

"I gave it to A-ken Sao. Her rent is overdue and she has not heard from A-ken for a whole year. She was about to drown herself."

"But what are we going to do? We don't have any

74

food in the house. Couldn't you at least have saved part of it for us?"

"I told her that it was from A-ken. If I hadn't, she would not have taken it."

"But are we supposed to starve in the new year? We can't go to bed with empty stomachs. You will have to go and borrow some money."

So Mr. Yeh went out to borrow money. He knew that New Year's Eve was the worst time to do such a thing—not only because people were busy cooking dinner, but also because they believed that borrowers could bring them bad luck in the new year. Almost every door was shut in Mr. Yeh's face, and when a man finally handed him a small package, all he got was some dirt wrapped in a piece of paper.

Tired and disappointed, Mr. Yeh went home. "Let's go to bed and not think about dinner," he said to Mrs. Yeh.

"I am too hungry to sleep," said his wife. "Can't you do something?"

"What do you want me to do?"

"At least you can get us some sweet potatoes from the fields."

"Those sweet potatoes don't belong to us."

"Come over, let me whisper into your ear."

Mr. Yeh leaned over.

"What? You want me to steal?"

"Shh, shh. Don't use that word. Say 'move.' "

"That's the same thing. I am not going to do it."

"Old man, are you going to starve us to death?" Mrs. Yeh began to cry.

Finally, Mr. Yeh decided that he had to "move" some sweet potatoes into their home whether he liked it or not. So he took a basket and a knife and walked toward the fields.

The sweet-potato field belonged to a widow, Liu Sao, and her only son, young Hsiao-pao. Now, Liu Sao knew that New Year's Eve was usually a good time for people to steal sweet potatoes, since she would be busy cooking the New Year's dinner. This year, Liu Sao decided to take extra precautions. She walked her son to the fields to stand guard and promised to relieve him when she finished cooking dinner.

Hsiao-pao settled down in the tent his mother had pitched in the fields. He blew out the lamp and sat in the darkness. If somebody was going to come and steal, Hsiao-pao had to catch the thief by surprise. He had a heavy stick almost as tall as himself, which he would use to strike the unwelcome visitor. It would be a blow that no thief could ever forget.

After a long wait, during which he nearly fell asleep more than once, he saw a tall figure creep surreptitiously into the small chapel at the edge of the field, where the T'u-ti P'u-sa—the Buddha of earth—was worshipped. "I'd better go and take a look," he said to himself. Since he was used to walking in the dark, he got into the temple and hid behind the altar in no time.

A man was kneeling in front of the altar. In the dim candlelight, Hsiao-pao was surprised to see that it was his former teacher, Mr. Yeh.

Kowtowing incessantly to the statue of T'u-ti P'u-sa, Mr. Yeh said, "T'u-ti P'u-sa, T'u-ti P'u-sa, tell me what I am supposed to do. A-ken Sao almost killed herself because A-ken didn't come home, so I gave her my silver *yüan-pao*. Now my wife and I are going to starve. My wife wants me to 'move' some sweet potatoes from the fields—do you think it is all right for me to do so? If you think so, please show me a sign." Mr. Yeh stood up, picked up the *ch'ien* holder from the altar, drew out two *ch'ien*, and threw them on the ground. Then he closed his eyes and prayed.

Ch'ien are fortune-telling sticks people use to seek advice when they are not sure what to do. The *ch'ien* have long and short lines engraved on each side. The way to work the *ch'ien* is to throw two or three on the ground and read the pattern they form. A certain pattern will represent a go-ahead sign.

When Hsiao-pao heard what Mr. Yeh was praying about, he laughed silently. "Let me play T'u-ti P'u-sa," he said to himself. While Mr. Yeh's eyes were still

77

closed, Hsiao-pao crawled under the altar and looked at the *ch'ien*. They did not form a go-ahead pattern. He quickly flipped one *ch'ien* over and crawled back under the altar.

Mr. Yeh opened his eyes, bent down, and looked at the *ch'ien*. They formed a go-ahead pattern. He smiled. "T'u-ti P'u-sa, you approved this. Thank you. But just to be sure, could you give me the sign one more time?" He threw two more *ch'ien* to the ground, closed his eyes, and prayed again.

Hsiao-pao, trying hard to keep from laughing aloud, crawled out to make sure that the *ch'ien* formed a go-ahead pattern.

"Go-ahead again!" cried Mr. Yeh. "Oh, T'u-ti P'u-sa. Please give me the sign once more. As soon as I get some money, I will buy incense to honor you." He worked the *ch'ien* again, and, of course, he was not disappointed.

"Thank you, T'u-ti P'u-sa," said Mr. Yeh reverently. "I promise to pay Liu Sao and Hsiao-pao back as soon I find a way to get some money." Mr. Yeh kowtowed three times and walked out of the temple, with Hsiao-pao quietly following him.

"Ha, teacher," Hsiao-pao laughed to himself, "you always told us that one should never steal, but today, you yourself are breaking the rule." He stayed quietly on the edge of the field and watched as Mr. Yeh put

down the basket he had brought with him and started to dig sweet potatoes with a knife.

Mr. Yeh was an excellent teacher but a terrible sweet-potato digger. He was so inexperienced and afraid of being discovered that he progressed very slowly. "T'u-ti P'u-sa," he cried again, "can't you give me some help?"

Hsiao-pao almost burst out laughing. "Good, let's have some more fun," he said to himself. He took out a knife and started to dig up sweet potatoes from the plants around him with amazing speed. Then he tossed them at Mr. Yeh. Sweet potatoes rained down on the old teacher, and some of them hit their target right on his forehead.

"T'u-ti P'u-sa, thank you, thank you," cried Mr. Yeh, "but don't go too fast, I can't keep up!"

Figuring that Mr. Yeh had had enough, the "little T'u-ti P'u-sa" stopped. Mr. Yeh picked up his basket and went home.

Soon after, when Liu Sao went to the fields to relieve her son, she found him away from his tent. Many holes in the field had been dug, and a lot of sweet potatoes were missing.

"Hsiao-pao, where are you?" she cried.

"Shh, shh . . . Here I am." Hsiao-pao crept out from the dark. "I was playing T'u-ti P'u-sa."

"T'u-ti P'u-sa? Look, so many sweet potatoes are gone. You must have been sleeping!"

"No, Mr. Yeh stole them," said Hsiao-pao with a mischievous smile.

"That's not a nice thing to say. Mr. Yeh is such a decent old gentleman."

"But it's true. And I helped him." Hsiao-pao told his mother the whole story.

"Poor Mr. Yeh. He must be having a hard time. Tomorrow morning let's go wish him a Happy New Year and take him some New Year food. He has always been so kind to you."

The next morning, Hsiao-pao and his mother went to wish Mr. Yeh and his wife a Happy New Year. As they were approaching the house, they were surprised to hear Mr. Yeh saying to Mrs. Yeh, "Old woman, help yourself, eat some *hung-shao-jou*," and Mrs. Yeh saying, "Old man, don't be shy, eat some cold sliced pork."

Hsiao-pao was very upset. "So Mr. Yeh was lying. If he has money to buy pork, why did he come to steal our sweet potatoes?"

"Shh, let's look," said his mother. They peeped through the window and saw Mr. Yeh putting a piece of red-skinned sweet potato into his wife's bowl as she was putting a white-skinned sweet potato into his bowl. They were both making believe that they were eating pork!

Hsiao-pao laughed and banged on the door. "Mr. Yeh, Mr. Yeh!"

Mr. Yeh sprang from his chair and looked at his wife. "Hsiao-pao is here!"

Mrs. Yeh quickly took away the remaining sweet potatoes, while Mr. Yeh looked for a place to hide the skins of the ones they'd eaten. He rushed over to the stove, threw the skins into a pot, and put the lid on.

Once in the house, Hsiao-pao knelt down and wished Mr. Yeh and his wife a Happy New Year. Mr. Yeh's face became very red when Liu Sao handed him the New Year food.

A minute later, A-ken Sao came in with her daughter, Ying-hua. "Thank you, Mr. Yeh, you saved us. Without the money you brought back to me, we would have been lost."

"So you are all here!" A voice behind them made them all turn around.

A-ken was standing by the door.

A-ken Sao was ecstatic. "A-ken, I came to thank Mr. Yeh for bringing me the money you sent me. Without it, Ying-hua would have been sold."

"What is this all about?" asked A-ken. "I never

asked Mr. Yeh to bring you any money." He looked confused.

"I know everything about this," said Hsiao-pao. And in a few sentences, he told the whole story.

A-ken and his wife fell on their knees. "Thank you, Mr. Yeh!" they said.

Hsiao-pao walked over to the stove. He took the lid off the pot where the sweet-potato skins were hidden. *"Hung-shao-jou!"* he exclaimed. Tossing them into the air, he laughed out loud.

The Miracle Doctor

About eighteen hundred years ago, there lived in China a doctor named Hua T'o. Using medicines he made from herbs, Hua T'o had saved thousands of people who were dying of incurable diseases. He was known as the "Miracle Doctor."

One hot and humid day, Hua T'o was traveling on the road and came across a man wailing beside a cart. Hua T'o walked up to the man, put his hand on his shoulder, and asked, "*Ta-ko*, what's the matter?"

"I've been struck by disaster," said the tearful man. "My daughter and I were on our way to visit some relatives when she suddenly became ill. There she is, lying in the cart. She is dead! I am sure she is dead!"

"Let me look at her," said Hua T'o. He gently lifted

the cloth that covered the girl's face, and examined her eyes. Then he felt her pulse. "Be of good cheer," he said to the man. "Your daughter is not dead. I can bring her back to consciousness."

Hua T'o took an acupuncture needle from his sack, pushed it deftly into the girl's scalp, and drew it out immediately. Then he broke a branch from a tree, stuck it into the ground, and said to the man, "When the shadow of the stick becomes one *ch'ih* long, your daughter will awaken." He then gathered up his things and continued on his way.

The man sat on the side of the road and waited anxiously. When the shadow of the stick became one *ch'ih* long, the girl opened her eyes.

"Where am I, Father?"

"My child, you almost died!" said the man. "Fortunately, a doctor came by and saved your life."

"A doctor? Where is he?" The girl's eyes followed her father's hand as he pointed to a small figure in the distance moving farther and farther away.

"It must be the Miracle Doctor!" she said.

A few days later, in a tavern on the side of a lonely road, Hua T'o was having a cup of tea. Two men sitting at a table in a corner were drinking heavily. One of them, who was in military uniform, took out a coin from his purse, tossed it on the table, and said to the tavern keeper, "Hey, fellow. Bring me another bottle of wine."

"I am sorry, sir," said the tavern keeper. "I am afraid that you have had too much to drink. Besides, I have only one bottle left, and I would like to save it for another customer."

"I'll drink and I'll pay," said the man. "But if you don't bring me the wine, you are not going to have a shop anymore."

The tavern keeper paled. Without another word, he brought the last bottle of wine over to the table.

The doctor saw everything. He picked up his walking stick, strode to the table where the two men were sitting, and, before the man in uniform had a chance to touch the bottle, he smashed it into pieces.

"Listen," he said to the man, "if you cherish your life, stay away from wine. You are seriously ill. If you stop drinking, you may have three more months to live. If you continue to drink, you will be dead in three days." He picked up his sack and walked out of the tavern, leaving the two men stunned.

The man in military uniform seemed to have sobered up a bit. He rose and said to his companion, "Let's get out of here!"

As the two walked out, the man said, "This crazy old man said that I am sick. Do I look like someone who is sick? I am strong!" To prove what he said, he marched a few steps, but his legs shook and he collapsed.

Three months later, Hua T'o was on the road again. As he neared a small town, he saw a young girl running toward him. When she reached him, she fell on her knees and said, "Miracle Doctor, I am so glad I found you. I have been trying to find you so I could thank you for saving my life."

"Are you sure I saved your life, my child?" said the doctor. "I don't remember treating you at all."

"Of course you did!" said the girl. "My name is Lan Ying. Three months ago my father and I were going to visit our relatives. I fell ill on the road and almost died. Luckily, you came by and saved my life. Surely you remember now?"

"Oh, now I do!" said Hua T'o. "I am so happy to see you well again. Where is your father, Lan Ying?"

"He is having a drink. Would you care to join us?" The girl pointed to a wine shop a few steps away.

"I would be glad to." The doctor followed the girl into the wine shop.

But as soon as he saw the girl's father, a strange look appeared on his face. "I am sorry, but I can't join you, *Ta-ko*. For your own good, stay away from wine." He quickly turned around and walked away.

The girl ran after him. "Doctor Hua, is there anything wrong?"

"Your father is seriously ill. He has a strange kind of disease that makes him allergic to wine. If he keeps on drinking, he will die very soon."

"Please do something!" cried Lan Ying. "You are the Miracle Doctor. You can treat any kind of disease!"

"I am very sorry," Hua T'o replied, shaking his head. "This is a deadly disease. So far, I have not found a cure for it. Please forgive me." And with a heavy heart he went away.

Hua T'o's wife was anxiously waiting for him at home. "We are in trouble," she said. "There is a military man waiting for you in the living room. He refuses to leave until he sees you."

As the doctor walked into the living room, the man rose and bowed deeply. "Doctor Hua, I came to thank you for saving my life," he said. "Three months ago you caught me drunk in a tavern, making a scene. You told me that I was terminally ill and should stop drinking right away. I did not believe you, but then I collapsed right after you left. Fortunately, I sought treatment, and now I am cured. I came to thank you. Now I must go."

"Wait," said the doctor. "I did not know there was a cure for this kind of disease. Can you tell me who treated you?"

"I was lucky," the man replied. "The tavern keeper told me that on Mount Lotus a monk could treat this kind of disease. So I went up there, got five balls made from magic herbs, and was cured." He bowed and left.

That night Hua T'o could not sleep at all. The tearful face of Lan Ying kept appearing in his mind. "Hua T'o, Hua T'o!" he said to himself. "You are unworthy of the name Miracle Doctor. Hundreds of people are dying of this terrible disease, and you can do nothing to stop it. You must go up the mountain to find out about the magic cure."

But that was no easy task. The doctor knew all too well that the monk would never give the secret formula of his herb medicine to an outsider. Hua T'o would have to become a monk first. So he changed his name to Hsüeh Fang and traveled to Mount Lotus.

The temple where the monk lived was halfway up Mount Lotus. When the doctor reached it, he saw a long line of people waiting their turn to go in and see the monk. Many of them were carried either on the back of a relative or on a stretcher.

When it was the doctor's turn, he walked into the temple and went straight up to a monk who was sitting on a cushion in front of the altar with his legs folded under his body. The doctor knelt down and began to say aloud, "Teacher, my name is Hsüeh Fang, and I am a homeless man. I have decided to let go all worldly desires and become a monk. Please allow me to be one of your disciples."

The monk closed his eyes and said slowly, "Not everyone can reach the height of holiness and become a monk, Hsüeh Fang. I think we can use you only as a cleaning person. We will give you food and a place to sleep."

So the doctor became a cleaning person. Every day he swept the grounds outside the temple, hoping for a chance to find out about the magic cure. But it was a closely guarded secret. The monk even denied that he used herbs to treat patients. "I am a monk, not a doctor," he said to his apprentices. "I don't believe in medicine. I heal people with the supernatural power I gained from years of prayer and sacrifice. Only the pure and the devout will be given such power."

And yet every day, when the doctor was sweeping the grounds outside the temple, he noticed that after the patients had been seen by the monk, they would always leave the temple with five wax balls in their hands. The doctor knew that the secret was contained in those wax balls. But whenever he asked a patient to let him look at them, the monk's oldest apprentice, Big Brother, would yell at him, "Don't stand there like that. Go back to work!" The doctor wasn't making any progress.

The monk had a younger apprentice, known as Little

Brother, who was more friendly. Every morning he would climb up to the top of the mountain and collect herbs. Several times the doctor offered to go with him, but Little Brother would always say, "No. You can't come with me. Teacher does not want anyone to know the kind of herbs I collect for him."

The doctor knew there was a special room in the south wing of the temple, but no one except the monk and Big Brother was allowed to go there. Every night, after the apprentices and the doctor had gone to bed, the monk would lock himself in the room for hours.

One night, the doctor tried to find out what the monk was doing. Thinking that the two apprentices were in bed, he quietly made his way to the south wing. From the shadow on the window paper he could see that the monk was stirring something in a pot on a stove. He smelled herbs but could not tell exactly what they were. As he stood there, he felt a hand grabbing his shoulder. It was Big Brother's.

"What are you doing, Hsüeh Fang?" Big Brother demanded. "How dare you come here! Go back to bed!"

Without uttering a word, the doctor obeyed.

A month passed. Hua T'o had still not learned the secret of the magic cure. But one day an opportunity came.

The monk happened to be out for a visit, and his

two apprentices were seeing patients inside the temple. As the doctor was sweeping the ground outside, he was surprised to see Lan Ying coming out of the temple with five wax balls in her hand. Behind her trudged a man carrying her father on his back. The doctor went up to Lan Ying and drew her aside.

"Lan Ying," he said softly.

Lan Ying was surprised. "What are you doing here, Doctor Hua?"

"Hush, don't call me Doctor," he said in a low voice. "People here know me only as a cleaning person. I came to find out the secret of the magic cure. I need your help. Please lend me one of the wax balls you have in your hand. I want to find out the ingredients in the medicine. Then I can make one exactly like this and return it to you."

Lan Ying hesitated. "I can't take the risk," she said. "Big Brother said that my father needs to take one ball a day for five consecutive days. If he misses one, he will die."

"My child," Lan Ying's father called. He had also recognized the doctor. "You can't say no to Doctor Hua. He saved your life. I trust him."

Slowly, the girl handed the doctor one of the wax balls. "Take it, Doctor. But please remember that my father's life depends on your returning it on time."

"I promise you I will make one exactly the same as

this and bring it to you on the fifth day," said Hua T'o. "Where are you staying?"

"We will be staying at an inn near the foot of the mountain."

"I will find you there," said the doctor.

The doctor ran back into his room and shut the door. He peeled off the wax and dissolved the herb ball in water. He dipped his finger in the mixture and tasted it.

"How strange! His formula is exactly the same as mine. We have been using the same kinds of herbs to treat that deadly disease, but why is it that my medicine doesn't work? Is it because the yellow flowers that grow on this mountain are more powerful than the ones I use?"

Suddenly the door flew open and Big Brother walked in. He snatched the bowl from the doctor's hands and looked at it. "So you came to steal the formula, you thief!" he cried. "Get out!" He spilled the medicine on the ground.

The doctor had no choice but to pick up his things and leave.

Little Brother, who had now become his friend, followed him sadly. Handing him a bunch of yellow flowers, he said, "Brother Hsüeh, I am so sorry to see you go. Here are some herbs I gathered this morning. Take them with you. You may need them."

Hui

The doctor thanked him and started to walk down the mountain. Just then he heard loud cries coming from the temple.

"Big Brother is possessed by the devil again," said Little Brother. "Don't worry about him. You'd better be on your way before Teacher gets back."

But Hua T'o rushed back into the temple. He saw Big Brother rolling on the floor, moaning. He checked the man's eyes, felt his pulse, and then pressed his abdomen. He could tell that the man was seriously ill and would die if he did not have surgery at once. But should he do it? He might not have time to get away before the monk came back.

"Get me some wine," he told Little Brother, who came in after him. Hua T'o took a paper package from his sack and poured the contents into the bowl of wine that Little Brother brought him. "Go out and keep a watch for Teacher. If you see him coming, cough loudly."

Hua T'o pried open Big Brother's mouth with a chopstick and forced the medicine down his throat. The man became still. The doctor took out a small knife and started to operate on the man's abdomen. Just when he finished the surgery he heard Little Brother coughing.

Hua T'o quickly covered the incision with a clean cloth, gathered his things and the bunch of yellow flowers, and hurried out of the temple, only to find himself face-to-face with the monk.

The monk looked at the yellow flowers in the doctor's hands. He snatched them away and said, "So I was right. I have always suspected that you were a quack doctor. And you came here to steal my secret formula."

"Yes, I am a doctor," said Hua T'o. "Are you not one? Are you not treating patients with herbal medicine just as we doctors do? Why do you refuse to share your secret when you want to save lives?"

The monk looked angry. "Leave at once," he ordered.

Disheartened, the doctor started down the mountain.

In the meantime, the monk walked into the temple and saw his big apprentice lying on the floor with a cloth covering his abdomen.

"Look," said Little Brother, "Big Brother has opened his eyes."

The monk took off the cloth and examined the incision. It was made perfectly. Only the hands of the most skillful doctor could have done that. He then picked up the bowl from the table, dipped his finger into the medicine, and tasted it.

"*Ma-fei-san!* This is the special kind of anesthetic the

Miracle Doctor Hua T'o uses in surgery. And yet Hsüeh Fang used it to save my apprentice's life! He must be the Miracle Doctor!"

Hua T'o was moving slowly down the mountain. "I have failed," he said to himself. Without the yellow flowers, he could not reproduce the medicine. What was he going to tell Lan Ying and her father when he saw them? How could he tell them that Lan Ying's father was going to die?

"Brother Hsüeh Fang! Brother Hsüeh Fang!" Little Brother called, running after him. In his hands he was holding a bag. "Teacher told me to give this to you."

The doctor opened the bag and found a note inside. It read: "Blossoming yellow flowers in March, useless weeds in April." What did that mean? He put his hand in the bag and took out a bunch of dried yellow flowers.

All of a sudden he knew! The secret was simple! The reason his medicine didn't work was because he had always used fresh yellow flowers collected in April, when they were fully grown. The medicine had by then spread into the leaves and no longer remained in the roots. The monk was telling him that to cure the strange disease he should use the dried roots of the yellow flowers that grew in March instead, because that was where the medicine was stored! The note in his hand held the secret of the cure for the deadly disease! He could hardly believe it.

The Miracle Doctor followed the monk's instructions and made the medicine. He saved many people from that strange disease. And the first one he saved, of course, was Lan Ying's father.

The Royal Bridegroom

It was close to midnight. In the wedding chamber of the Royal Palace, Princess Yün-hua, sitting by the side of her bed, let forth a deep sigh. She had been there since the wedding ceremony, and the red silk veil covering her head was making her very uncomfortable. Although she could not see anybody through the veil, she knew that her *kung-o*—her maids-in-waiting—had already withdrawn to their quarters and she was alone with the bridegroom, her *fu-ma*.

The princess was glad at least that the wedding ceremony was over. It had been such a long one, and since her head was covered by the veil the whole time, she had to do everything with the help of her *kung-o*, as though she were blindfolded. She never even got a chance to see her *fu-ma*'s face and wondered if he was as attractive as the emperor, her brother, had said. Anyway, she knew she was going to find out soon.

As she sat there, she heard a deep sigh. Fu-ma must be tired, too. She lifted her veil and peeped out. Fu-ma had risen from the place where he had been sitting and was pacing back and forth across the room. Then he turned around, and she saw his face. How handsome he was! So her brother, the emperor, was right! But why didn't Fu-ma come to take off her veil? It was time for them to have their private toast. What was bothering him?

Finally, the princess could not wait any longer. She decided to break the rules and take off the veil herself. Putting it aside, she called out to her *fu-ma*, who, for some reason, had stopped pacing. He was sitting down on a chair.

"Fu-ma, this is our wedding night. Let's have a toast," the princess said gently.

"Serve the wine," Fu-ma ordered arrogantly.

The princess was shocked. She had never expected Fu-ma to be so rude. Nevertheless, she filled a cup with wine and brought it over to Fu-ma, who gulped it down.

"Another cup," he ordered.

The princess was perplexed. How dare he behave like this? But she didn't want a quarrel on her wedding night, so she suppressed her resentment, filled the cup a second time, and handed it to Fu-ma. Again, Fu-ma drank it off without waiting for a toast.

"Fill up the cup," he ordered for a third time.

The princess could control her anger no longer. She put the wine pitcher down on the table. "Fu-ma, how dare you order me about like a servant. Please remember that I am a princess."

"But now you have become my wife. You should follow my rules," said Fu-ma without even looking at her.

"Your rules?" The princess was astounded.

"Yes. My rules. Every morning you should get up before I do. Lay out my clothes and my shoes. Make sure my tea is made properly and my meals are well cooked."

"I have never done those things before!" cried the princess.

"It's high time you learned," Fu-ma continued. "And that is not all. You must give me a son within a year. If you don't, I will divorce you."

"Divorce me? You wouldn't dare!" The princess was outraged.

"Why not? This is the law of heaven and earth. If you fail to give birth to a son, you will be divorced."

"What if I have a daughter?"

"A daughter? If you give birth to a daughter, you

will be asked to take your own life. Your job is to produce an heir. If you fail to do so, you shall die. That will save you from disgrace."

"Let's see if you dare ask me to do such a thing! I am going to talk to my brother right now; he will have your head cut off!" the princess retorted vehemently. She stood up and was about to summon her maids to accompany her to see the emperor.

"Not so fast!" said Fu-ma. He threw back his head and laughed. "I was only joking. All I wanted was to show you the kind of life ordinary women live. You are a princess. You have always been waited upon hand and foot, so you have no sympathy for ordinary women at all."

"How do you know?" asked the princess. She felt insulted.

"Well, I can prove that later. But, first, let me tell you a story." Fu-ma suddenly seemed to be in good humor.

"There was once a high official who wanted a son so badly, he warned his wife that she would be asked to take her life if she gave birth to a daughter. The woman was terrified. When she did give birth to a girl, she wrote to her husband in the capital and told him she had given birth to a boy. The official was delighted. The girl was dressed like a boy and brought up as a boy. She learned to read and write and proved to be just as intelligent as any boy could be. At the age of eighteen, she was summoned by her father to the capital to take the imperial examinations. She did so well that she was selected by the emperor himself to be the *chuang-yüan* of the year."

"Unbelievable!" the princess exclaimed.

"But soon trouble began. High officials in the imperial court began to propose marriage on behalf of their daughters. She turned down all the proposals. But when the emperor issued a royal decree granting her the hand of the daughter of one of his highest officials, she knew she could no longer refuse, or she would be punished."

"Then what did she do?" asked the princess.

"She had to obey the decree and go through the wedding ceremony. Can you imagine how she felt afterward, when she was left alone for the first time in the wedding chamber with her bride? On the other hand, what would you have done if you were that high official's daughter and discovered on your wedding night that your bridegroom was in fact a woman?"

"I don't believe that really happened," said the princess. "If it did happen, though, I would forgive that woman and ask my father, the high official, to beg the emperor to pardon the woman for disguising herself as a man."

"Do you really mean it?" asked Fu-ma.

"Of course I do. I am a princess. I always mean what I say."

Fu-ma let out a sigh of relief as he dropped to his knees. "Princess, I am that woman!"

"No," cried the princess. "This can't be true!"

"Why not?" asked Fu-ma.

"Because if you are a woman, then I don't have a husband anymore. If you are a woman, I am going to kill you!" The princess reached for a sword that was hanging on the wall.

"Princess, you said that you would forgive the woman and ask the emperor to grant her pardon."

"Yes, I said that because I didn't know you were that woman," the princess said angrily.

"You said you always meant what you said," Fu-ma reminded her.

"I said that because I didn't know you were that woman."

"Princess, don't you have any sympathy for an ordinary woman?" said Fu-ma sadly.

"Ordinary woman! Ordinary woman! Does an ordinary woman have a wedding night like this?" The princess was almost in tears. "Even if I can forgive you," she continued, "my brother, the emperor, will not. Don't you know that it is a mortal offense for a woman to disguise herself as a man and set foot in the palace? You have cheated the emperor, and this is a

crime that cannot be pardoned. Once your true identity is revealed, it will become a scandal in the palace, and you will be put to death in no time."

"Princess, please let me go," pleaded Fu-ma.

"Go? Where can you go? The palace is strictly guarded, and nobody can leave at night. Tomorrow we are expected to appear as a newlywed couple in front of the emperor and greet the well-wishers. If you depart without an explanation, my brother will feel so insulted that I am sure he will issue an imperial decree to have you arrested. No matter where you go, you will be found. There is no place for you to hide. I can't pretend all my life that I am married to you; I don't want to kill you; I can't keep you here. Oh! What am I going to do with you?" The princess burst into tears.

A faint smile appeared on Fu-ma's face. "Princess, there is a way," she said calmly.

"What is it?" asked the princess as she took out a red silk handkerchief to wipe away her tears.

"Don't you know the saying 'cook it the same way'?" asked Fu-ma.

" 'Cook it the same way'?" the princess repeated.

"Yes. When I told you the story about that woman, it was easy for you to forgive her because you didn't know you were also part of the story. If we 'cook it the same way' and tell the emperor the same story, maybe he will pardon me."

"That's a wonderful idea!" cried the princess. "And I guess I know how to tell it to make sure he will be moved. I think that you are very clever. I wish you really were my husband! What a pity! Well, now I think it is time for bed. I am quite tired." The two blew out the candles and retired for the night.

The next morning, the emperor summoned all his high officials to the palace. He wanted to introduce his sister and her new husband to them.

"The Princess *Ch'ien-sui* and Fu-ma!" announced a eunuch.

The princess, dressed in a beautiful long pink dress, walked in with her husband, who was wearing a robe of a similar color. Fu-ma's father smiled proudly at his "son," who ignored him. The princess and Fu-ma went down on their knees and wished the emperor good health.

"Rise, my dear sister and Fu-ma," said the emperor. He was delighted, thinking that he had found the perfect husband for his sister. "Did you sleep well?"

"In fact, we spent the whole night talking," said the princess. "Fu-ma told me the most incredible story I have ever heard."

"That's wonderful. Be seated, my dear sister, and you, too, Fu-ma. Let's all hear the story."

"A girl was brought up as a boy because her father did not want a daughter," the princess began. "Her identity was kept a secret from the moment she was born. She learned everything a boy would learn, and she was as intelligent as any boy could be."

"That is hard to believe!" said the emperor, listening with interest.

"Well, when she was eighteen, her father, an official in the imperial court, told her to go to the capital and take the imperial examinations. She finished with flying colors and was selected by the emperor to be *chuang-yüan*. Besides this, the emperor gave the daughter of his defense minister to her in marriage."

"What a fool that emperor was!" exclaimed the princess's brother. "I cannot imagine how he could have failed to distinguish a woman from a man. How did the story end?"

"Well, when the woman's identity was finally revealed, the emperor felt that since he was the one who had made the mistake, he should be responsible for it. So he pardoned the woman. But he did more than that. He was so impressed by her talent, he adopted her as his sister."

"That's a delightful story," said the emperor. "I love the happy ending."

"Would *Wan-sui* do the same if it really happened to you?" asked the princess.

"Of course. Why not?" the emperor said, without thinking.

Fu-ma dropped to her knees. "I thank *Wan-sui* for his mercy!"

The emperor was astounded. "What does this mean?" he demanded.

"I am a woman," said Fu-ma.

The emperor flew into a rage. "How dare you cheat your emperor! How dare you set foot on the sacred steps of the imperial palace. Guards, take her out and behead her!"

The imperial guards rushed over and were about to lay their hands on the woman. But there was a loud cry in the court: Fu-ma's father had fainted.

Fu-ma stood up. "An emperor never plays with his words. *Wan-sui* has already granted me pardon, and he cannot go back on his word."

"That's right," said the princess. "Also, if Fu-ma is beheaded, I will become a widow, since legally we are still married."

The whole court became very quiet. Everyone was waiting for the emperor to say something.

Finally, after a period of silence, the emperor let out a laugh. "I didn't realize that I was making a fool of myself. You are right, my dear sister. I am responsible for all this. Well, I guess I have no choice but to do what was done in the story. Yes, I will pardon Fu-ma and make her my sister. As for you, my dear sister, the marriage will be annulled, and I will find another fine young man to be your husband."

"Thank you, *Wan-sui*!" cried the princess and Fu-ma as they went down on their knees again.

So Fu-ma became the emperor's adopted sister. A week later, the two princesses were married to two fine young officials in a joint wedding ceremony presided over by the emperor himself.

Pronunciation Guide

Note: I have chosen the Wade-Giles system to romanize Chinese names and terms. In the Wade-Giles system, an apostrophe is used to indicate when certain consonants are to be aspirated: for instance, *Ch'in* is pronounced "chin" while *Chin* is "jin." Also, in Wade-Giles, *ü* indicates a sound like the letter "u" in French.

A-ken Sao: ah-ghen sao
Chang Chen: jang jen
Chang T'ien-shih: jang tien-sh ("sh" prolonged)
Chao: jao
Chekiang: juh-jiang
Ch'en: chen
Ch'eng-shiang: cheng-shiang

Ch'i: chee
ch'ien: chien
Ch'ien-sui: chien-sway
ch'ih: ch (prolonged)
ch'i-lin: chee-lin
Chin: jin
Ch'in: chin
Ching: jing
Ch'ing: ching
Chou: joe
Ch'u: choo
chuang-yüan: jwang-yüan
Chui-yü: jwai-yü
Feng Meng-lung: fung meng-loong
fu-ma: foo-mah
Han: han
Ho-shih: huh-sh ("sh" prolonged)
Hsia hsiu-ts'ai kuo-nien: shia shiou-tsai gwoh-nien
Hsiang-ling: shiang-ling
Hsiao-pao: shiau-bao
Hsi-ch'ü: shee-chü
Hsien-yang: shien-yahng
Hsüeh Fang: shüeh fahng
Hsüeh Hsiang-ling: shüeh shiang-ling
hua-chiao: hwah-jiau
hua-pen: hwah-bun
Hua T'o: hwah twuh

hung-shao-jou: hoong-shao-roe
Kiangsu: jiang-soo
Kuan Han-ch'ing: gwan han-ching
Kuan-yin: gwan-yin
kung-o: goong-uh
Lai-chou: lie-joe
Lan Ying: lan ying
Lao-yeh: lau-yeh
li: lee
Li: lee
liang: liang
Lien P'o: lien po
Lin Hsiang-ju: lin shiang-roo
Liu Sao: lyou sao
Lo Kuan-chung: luo gwan-joong
Lu: loo
ma-fei-san: mah-fay-san
Meng Ch'ang: meng chang
men-k'o: men-kuh
Miao Hsien: miau shien
Mien-ch'ih: mien-ch ("ch" prolonged)
Mu: moo
Nü-chung-lang: nü-joong-lang
Pao Ch'eng: bao cheng
Pao Kung: bao goong
pa-pao-fan: bah-bao-fan
pa-pao-ts'ai: bah-bao-tsai

Pien Ho: bien huh
Pien-liang: bien-liang
San-kuo yen-i: san-gwoh yen-yi
Sao: sao
se: suh
Shanghai: shang-hai
Shao-hsing-hsi: shao-shing-shee
sheng-ssu-chih-chiao: sheng-ss-jh-jao ("ss" prolonged)
Shui-hu: shway-hoo
So-lin-nang: swoh-lin-nang
ssu-ch'üan: ss-chüan ("ss" prolonged)
Sung: soong
ta-hsi-jih-tzu: dah-shee-rur-dz ("dz" prolonged)
T'ai-tzu: tie-dz ("dz" prolonged)
Ta-jen: dah-run
Ta-ko: dah-guh
T'ang: tang
Ta-wang: dah-wang
Teng-chou: dung-joe
Tung-chou lieh-kuo chih: doong-joe lieh-gwoh jh ("jh"
   prolonged)
T'u-ti P'u-sa: too-dee poo-sah
Wan-sui: wan-sway
Wei: way
Wei Jan: way ran
Wen: wen
Wu: woo

wu-kung: woo-goong
Yeh: yeh
Yen: yen
Ying-hua: ying-hwah
Yüan: yüan
Yüan-hsiao: yüan-shiau
yüan-pao: yüan-bao
Yüan-wai: yüan-why
Yü Ch'ing: yü ching
Yüeh: yüeh
Yün-hua: yün-hwah
Yu-yang: yo-yahng

Glossary

Chang T'ien-shih: a deity known for his ability to expel demons and spirits

Ch'en: a term used by an official to refer to himself when talking to the emperor

Ch'eng-shiang: prime minister

ch'ien: fortune-telling sticks made of bamboo or wood

Ch'ien-sui: a term used to address members of an emperor's family, equivalent to "Your Royal Highness"

ch'ih: a unit of Chinese measurement that equals about thirteen inches *chuang-yüan*: the first-place winner of the imperial examinations

fu-ma: the husband of a princess; also used as an address

imperial examinations: examinations to select young men to become high officials

Jade Emperor: a powerful deity who rules the heavens

kowtow: a body gesture—usually kneeling and then touching the ground with one's forehead—that shows one's submissive reverence. According to the Wade-Giles system, the word should be spelled "k'o-t'ou"; however, since it has been widely accepted in the West as "kowtow," I have decided to retain this form

Kuan-yin: a compassionate Buddha who is considered the savior of the poor and the suffering

Lao-yeh: respectful form of address to a man who is wealthy or is a high official

li: a unit of length that equals five hundred meters

liang: a unit of weight for precious metals that equals approximately one ounce

ma-fei-san: a special kind of anesthetic invented by Hua T'o (?–208)

men-k'o: permanent houseguests of a wealthy man or a high official who lived in his house and served him with their skills in exchange for room, board, and a stipend

Peking opera: one of the major schools of Chinese opera, dating back almost two hundred years. Peking opera is known for its singing, gestures, monologues, and *wu-kung* (martial arts), and draws heavily on mime. It inherited many traditional stories from storytelling texts and from scripts by the great playwright Kuan Han-ch'ing, who flourished during the Yüan Dynasty (1271–1368)

Sao: literally means "sister-in-law," but is also used to address married women in the neighborhood

T'ai-tzu: crown prince

Ta-jen: a term a commoner used to address an official

Ta-ko: literally, "big brother"; often used to address a man whom one did not know personally

Ta-wang: a term used by a subject to address the king, equivalent to "Your Majesty"

Wan-sui: literally, "ten thousand years" (long life); a term used to address the emperor exclusively, equivalent to "Your Majesty"

Warring States (475–221 B.C.): an important period in Chinese history, during which the kings of several states under the reign of the sovereigns of the Chou Dynasty made war on one another

Yüan-hsiao Festival: the fifteenth day of the new year and the last day of the New Year celebration

yüan-pao: a bar of precious metal, usually made of gold or silver

Yüan-wai: esquire, gentleman, sometimes used as part of a name, such as in "The Ch'i-lin Purse"

Yüeh: a kind of regional opera that originated in Chekiang province toward the end of the Ch'ing Dynasty (1644–1912). It was later introduced into Shanghai and Kiangsu province. Originally known as *Shao-hsing-hsi*, the opera's name was changed to Yüeh in 1942. Yüeh is the name of a state during the Spring, Autumn, and Warring States period (770–221 B.C.) whose territory is now part of Chekiang and Kiangsu provinces. Drawing from many regional art forms and singing styles, the Yüeh tradition is nearly one hundred years old. For many years the opera actors were all women, but after 1949 male actors were also cast

Sources

"The Ch'i-lin Purse": From the Peking opera *So-lin-nang* (*The Purse That Locked the Ch'i-lin*), set in the Northern Sung Dynasty (960–1127). I have eliminated a final twist found in the original story: Hsiang-ling's husband and little boy find their way to Mr. Lu's home; but when the husband sees his wife now dressed in silk, he thinks she has become Mr. Lu's concubine and he gets very angry. After Mrs. Lu explains what has happened, the two are reconciled. (Strictly speaking, "ch'i-lin" should be spelled "ch'i-ling." I chose "lin" to differentiate it from the character Hsiang-ling.)

"Dog Steals and Rooster Crows": From *Tung-chou lieh-kuo chih* (*The States of Tung-chou*), a historical novel compiled by Ming Dynasty writer Feng Meng-lung (1574–1646), which deals with many important events from the Spring, Autumn, and Warring States period (770–221 B.C.). The proverbial expression "Rooster crows and Dog steals" originated from this story. Unfortunately, in modern Chinese the expression has a pejorative implication—"bad company"—which in no way does justice to the theme of the story.

"The Two Miss Peonys": From the Chinese Yüeh opera *Chui-yü* (*The Carp-fish Chase*), set in the Northern Sung Dynasty. The imperial investigator Pao Ch'eng (999–1062), known as Pao Kung, was famous for his uprightness and shrewdness in solving difficult criminal cases.

"The Ho-shih Jade": From *Tung-chou lieh-kuo chih*. The Ho-shih Jade was discovered in the state of Ch'u by a man named Pien Ho, who in 757 B.C. offered the stone first to King Li. The king thought it was a fake and ordered Pien Ho's left foot cut off as punishment. In 740 B.C. Pien Ho offered the stone to King Wu, who also thought it was a fake and had Pien Ho's right foot cut off. In 689 B.C., after King Wen ascended the throne, he learned that Pien Ho was weeping at the base of Mount Ching with the stone in his arms. The king sent his servant to ask him why he was weeping. Pien Ho replied, "I am not weeping because I lost my two feet, I am weeping because the kings called this priceless treasure a fake and I was punished for telling the truth." The king ordered his jeweler to evaluate the stone. The craftsman opened up the stone and found the jade inside. The jade was then recognized as a genuine treasure and named the Ho-shih Jade, which means "Ho's jade." The idiomatic expression "The entire jade returns to Chao" came from this story and is often used to promise that a borrowed item will be returned in its original condition.

"The Prime Minister and the General": From *Tung-chou lieh-kuo chih*. "The Ho-shih Jade" and "The Prime Minister and the General" are two parts of a long story. The proverbial expression "carrying a piece of wood to apologize" comes from this story and characterizes an apology made in a humble manner.

"The Clever Magistrate": The idea for this story was borrowed from a legend about Lo Kuan-chung (1330–1400), who wrote the famous historical novel *San-kuo yen-i* (*The Three Kingdoms*). I have taken great liberties in my retelling.

"Mr. Yeh's New Year": From the Yüeh opera *Hsia hsiu-ts'ai kuo-nien* (*Scholar Hsia Celebrates New Year*). The date of the original story is unknown. Since the Sung and Ming Dynasties are the two popular historical periods in which many Chinese opera stories are set, I have chosen to set this story in the Ming Dynasty.

"The Miracle Doctor": From a legend about Hua T'o (?–208), a famous doctor who lived at the end of the Eastern Han Dynasty (25–220). He was known for developing an anesthetic for surgery called *ma-fei-san*, and he also wrote several valuable books on Chinese medicine.

"The Royal Bridegroom": From the Yüeh opera *Nü-chung-lang* (*Man in a Woman*), and set in the Ming Dynasty for the same reason as "Mr. Yeh's New Year."